Had the dog gotten the wallet from the murderer? Or from Hank's body in the park?

The park. The mystery of the park's yellow tape was solved, but why question Zac? A paperboy. "Wait a minute, Carly. If Hank's been murdered, it's only natural they'd want to talk to his employees, right?"

She looked at me as if I had two heads. "You think that's it? That they're talking to all the people who work at the newspaper?"

"I'm sure of it."

She sank back against the seat and covered her face with her hands. "I was afraid that they'd found out about Atlanta."

Death on a Deadline

A Sleuthing Sisters Mystery

Sandy Gaskin
Christine Lynxwiler
Jan Reynolds

HEARTSONG
PRESENTS
MYSTERIES

Dedicated to our parents, H. B. Pearle and Ermyl McFadden Pearle, who taught us to love each other, to love books, and to strive to achieve our dreams. And to our other siblings, Kenny Pearle, Lynda Sampson, and Vicky Daughety, with whom we share childhood memories and, more importantly, a bond that can never be broken.

To Steve, Bart, and Kevin—three amazing husbands—for your patience with giggly all-night plotting sessions and not-so-giggly all-night writing sessions. To our incredible kids—Jacob, Megan, Jessa, Kristianna, and Kaleigh—thanks for the inspiration and support you've given us!

Thanks also to our golf expert, Clint Creecy.

One Final Dedication:
In memory of a steadfast man of God who touched
our lives and hearts in many ways:
Raymond Hanley—1938–2006

ISBN 978-1-59789-481-4

Cover design: Kirk DouPonce, DogEared Design
Cover illustration: Jody Williams

Our mission is to publish and distribute inspirational products offering exceptional value and biblical encouragement to the masses.

Printed in the U.S.A.

1

> ## Lake View Monitor
>
> ### HELP WANTED
>
> Early morning paper route available. Good pay. Must have dependable vehicle. Apply in person at the *Lake View Monitor* office, 243 Main St.

Hey! Dog! Stop digging up the yard!" I waved my arms wildly.

Mama had predicted more than once that curiosity would be my downfall. The instant I let that dog's incessant barking propel me out of bed, my fate was as sealed as the proverbial curious cat's. Especially once I peeked through the living room blinds and ran out on the porch, long Mickey Mouse gown flapping in the September breeze.

The startled golden retriever scooped up a brownish object in his mouth and galumphed down the sidewalk toward downtown. I squinted into the rainy mist. Was that my missing Dooney & Bourke wallet clutched in his teeth? I was off the porch and halfway down my driveway before I even realized my bare feet were splashing cold water against my legs.

The dog turned back for a split second as if to confirm I was behind him, then picked up the pace to a quick trot. We'd almost reached the city park—mercifully without seeing another human—and I was gaining on the dog when he looked back again. My brain finally kicked into gear. I was playing right into his hands. . .um, paws. I halted in my tracks.

He skidded to a stop. I dropped to my knees in a shallow puddle of water, but I managed to hold out a friendly-looking hand. *See? No threat here, buddy,* I thought with clenched teeth. "Here, doggy, doggy." Okay, so I have a cat, but how much different can it be? Apparently not much, because the golden retriever did that head-tilt thing and then sidled back to me, still clutching the brown object in his teeth.

"Give it to me, buddy."

To my shock, he dropped the slobbery wallet into my outstretched hand. *Ugh.* It wasn't a Dooney & Bourke. It wasn't even a Dooney & Bourke knockoff. This billfold was plain brown wet leather. I held it between my finger and thumb and flicked it open. A familiar face stared up at me from the Arkansas driver's license inside the flap. Hank Templeton, hard-hitting editor of the *Lake View Monitor*. Hank the Crank, people not as nice as me called him behind his back. Even I had to admit he could easily be a founding member of the Grumpy Old Men Society, if there were such a thing.

His wife, Marge, was probably wringing her hands

and trying to convince him she hadn't misplaced his wallet. I felt sorry for her. But not enough to show up at her door dressed like this. I'd do my good deed and take it by their house on my way to work.

I wrapped my arms around myself and bent my head against the wind. As I trudged through the rain, the retriever matched me step for step. "Shoo. Go home."

The collarless dog ignored my words. So I returned the favor and ignored his presence as I hurried home. My house came into view—slightly run-down, barely above low rent, but the light in the window beckoned like a flag at the finish line. And a hot shower would be my trophy.

Almost to the driveway. The hum of a motor behind me interrupted my mental victory dance. I quickened my pace. Maybe if I didn't look at the driver, he wouldn't notice me.

After all, why would he notice inconspicuous me? Barefoot in my nightgown? Oh, and how could I forget? The dog. Stuck to my side like a stray sock to a pair of rayon running shorts fresh from the dryer. The car slowed. *Please, please, please be a total stranger needing directions to the diner.*

The horn blew directly behind my right ear, and I turned instinctively. Great. Brendan Stiles. My date for tomorrow night.

He rolled down his window. "Hey, Jenna. Out for a stroll?" Dark hair and eyes, nice smile, even those cute little wire-rim glasses that made him look geeky but handsome. The local pharmacist and I had dated three times in the last month or so. The last two Sundays, he'd even shown up at church. Seemed ideal on the surface. Especially once I'd gotten used to covering his stingy tips for the waitress and overlooking the fact that he monopolized the conversation most of the time. But so far—big shock—no chemistry, at least on my part. And after seeing me today with no makeup and my hair frizzed out, probably no chemistry on his part, either. A fact over which I couldn't work up a great deal of distress.

I held up my soggy prize. "Had to see a dog about a wallet."

At his quizzical look, I spilled the whole story.

He laughed. In a nice way. "Want me to drop it off at Hank's office?"

"That's okay. I'll take it by the house." This was the most helpful I'd ever seen him. Maybe there was still hope.

"You sure? I'm going right by there. Why don't you let me take it?"

Okay, I'm cranky before I get my coffee, but he had just crossed over the line from helpful into obnoxiously persistent. *Never doubt your first instincts.*

"Thanks anyway."

"Have it your way. See you tomorrow night." He sped away.

I jogged up the driveway and slipped into the house, closing the door firmly against the dog's nose. A girl has to draw the line somewhere. I'd already been adopted by a neurotic cat that had to go to work with me every day because she couldn't stand to be alone.

On the way to work, I stopped at Hank and Marge's but got no answer in spite of my relentless doorbell ringing. I jumped back in the car, determined to make up my lost time. Hard to do, since my boss's long-ago run-in with the zoning committee had forced him to build outside the city limits. As I negotiated the crooks and turns of the hilly road, I thought about Brendan's easy acceptance of my wild appearance and felt a pang of guilt that I'd been less than impressed with him. Again.

I pulled into the Lake View Athletic Club parking lot, not as early as usual but with minutes to spare. Two women jogged in place outside the door in matching hot pink T-shirts and tight black leggings. Against the cream-colored siding of the building, they looked like oversized flamingos.

They were obviously newbies—their eagerness gave them away, as well as the T-shirts, still new-looking, straight from the club's sports shop, my name in big letters on the back. With my strawberry blond hair, I wouldn't be caught dead in hot pink, but thankfully, Bob doesn't make me wear the shirts. Just sell them.

No matter how much my boss insists we have to capitalize on my name, I'll never get used to seeing GET IN THE SWIM WITH JENNA STAFFORD emblazoned across the backs of perfect strangers or, worse still, people I know. Talk about cheesy. I *am* Jenna Stafford, and I don't even have a T-shirt with my name on it. But they sell like hotcakes, and I get a percentage of the profits in addition to my meager salary.

From the pink ladies' disgruntled looks, they'd counted on my habit of opening early. They should have been glad it was my day to open and not Gail's. The college student was always late. But they weren't looking for reasons to be glad.

Nothing starts a morning off better than dealing with a couple of irritated flamingos. Unless it's chasing a dog through the rain in your nightgown. Surely the day could only go up from here.

I clutched the cat carrier in one hand and unlocked the door, flipping on light switches as I went.

As the ladies followed me down the hallway past the U-shaped receptionist station and deserted smoothie bar, I stared straight ahead, praying they wouldn't mention the pictures that adorned the walls—a much younger me at various swim meets. Bob's insistence, again.

For about two months, at the tender age of sixteen, I'd been America's Olympic darling. Even though I left Lake View for college two years later and didn't move back for nearly a decade, the local residents still remember my summer of fame. Or shame, depending on how much stock you put into winning. Hence the booming T-shirt sales. Which proves that under Bob Pryor's good-ole-boy exterior beats the heart of a shrewd businessman.

I wouldn't call him a vulture, but when I gave up teaching and moved back to Lake View three years ago, he showed up with a job offer before my suitcases were unpacked. The position didn't pay much more than flipping burgers, but being able to swim every day in any weather was incentive enough. And his promise to retire in a couple of years and sell me the health club at a reasonable price had sealed the deal. Plus it saved me the humiliation of pounding the pavement in my old hometown. And of admitting my failures.

Those "couple of years" were up, though, and lately I suspected my boss had been avoiding my offers to buy the business. Even his current Caribbean cruise with Wilma smacked more of a need to elude me than of a need to re-spark the romance in his forty-year marriage. But with him gone, at least I would have the office to myself. Which worked for my Greta Garbo mood.

Unfortunately, the office stayed deserted as the day flew by in a blur of small problems and needy members. I didn't even get to darken the office door until four, when I finally nabbed a bottle of water from my little fridge and sank into my chair. Neuro jumped up on my walnut desk, rubbing her bumpy yellow fur against my arm, purring loudly. "Come here, you." I cradled her in my arms and relaxed.

Hayley, my ten-year-old niece, burst into the room. As she slammed down in the chair across from my desk, arms crossed, Neuro skittered off my lap and disappeared behind the file cabinet.

"Having a good day, I see."

"Mom's out there in the hallway." Hayley spat out the words. "Signing *us* up for gymnastics."

"You and Rachel don't want to take gymnastics anymore?"

She gave me the are-you-a-total-moron? look ten-year-olds do best. "*Rachel* wants to."

"Oh." Poor Carly. The twins had been identical, not only in looks, but in likes, for so long that we all tended to think of them as one entity.

A tap on the door interrupted our meaningful aunt-niece communication. "Hayley, sugar, there you are. I figured I'd find you in here." Carly gave me a distracted grin. "Hey, Jenna."

My sister brought her focus back to the still-scowling Hayley. "Can you do me a favor and go tell Rachel I'm in Aunt Jenna's office? She's down by the sign-up sheets."

Hayley rolled her eyes and mumbled something I couldn't quite make out.

"Don't give me that attitude, young lady," Carly said, drawing herself up to her full five feet two inches.

Hayley left with no more mumbling, and Neuro immediately scampered out of her hiding place. That cat can sense a mood better than most people I know.

"Help." Carly plopped into the chair her daughter had vacated. "Mama's words keep comin' out of my mouth."

I nodded. "When you said 'young lady,' I cringed and ducked."

"You notice Hayley didn't. I try to be tough, but I'll never have my bluff in on them like Mama did us." My sister is a wonderful mother with enough insecurity to keep a therapist busy for life. She's always been a little unsure of herself, but as a single mom raising three kids, she often falls prey to self-doubt.

"Are you going to make Hayley take gymnastics this year?" I kept my voice neutral. I'd seen so many miserable kids whose parents signed them up for classes they didn't want to take, but I couldn't make Carly's decisions for her.

"Who knows? I didn't end up puttin' her name on the list." She sighed. "I remember when I was eleven, Mama and Daddy let me quit swimming. I felt like *I'd* won the Olympics."

That was the year I'd turned seven. I'd already taken top prize in several competitions by then. A recurring thought surfaced for the gazillionth time. *Was I the cause of my big sister's lack of confidence in her abilities?*

"I swear those girls of mine are gonna be the death of me. I could've kissed Mama's feet when she offered to babysit tonight."

In spite of my tiredness, I grinned. How did my sister end up with such a soft Southern drawl? We were both born and raised in Lake View, Arkansas, and everyone around here says "y'all." But Carly takes it a step further. She lived in Atlanta for several years, and now she drops her *g*'s and softens her *r*'s like she's a native Georgian. Must be the *Gone with the Wind* effect. Turns every woman within a hundred-mile radius into Scarlett O'Hara.

"I'll get off work in about an hour. Why don't you come by the house after you take the kids home and we'll go get a bite to eat?"

"I thought you'd never ask." Carly ran her fingers through her short dark curls—a nervous habit that gives her a perpetually tousled look, reminiscent of a fifties starlet. But I knew that underneath that Betty Boop exterior beat a Betty Crocker heart. "Can you guarantee there won't be any ten-year-olds there?"

"C'mon, Car. This fighting won't last forever. By the time Hayley and Rachel are in high school, they'll be best friends again."

"Ya think?" She relaxed in her chair. Neuro took Carly's chilled-out posture as an invitation and leaped into her lap.

Carly pushed the cat off, but Neuro bounced back up like a Super Ball. She pushed again; Neuro bounced up again. "I give up, Baldy," she muttered.

"Hey. . ." I snatched Neurosis off her lap. "Cut the name-calling. She has a problem. But we're working on it."

"She's a cat," Carly drawled, making *cat* two syllables. "A cat that pulls her hair out. How do you work on that? Kitty therapy?"

Covering Neuro's ears with my hands, I dropped my voice to a whisper. "She only does it when she's alone. So I'm trying not to leave her alone much." The cat wiggled her head out from under my hands.

"Oh!" Carly sat straight up in her chair. "The weirdest thing happened earlier."

"What?"

"After I picked the girls up at school, they begged to go to Dairy King. I'm tellin' you, Jen, there's a secret ingredient in school lunches, programmed to fizzle out at exactly three o'clock. Remember how Mama used to have milk and cookies ready when we'd get off the bus? Anyway, I caved."

So far, so normal. My sister could never tell anything straight out. You had to drag it out of her in bits and pieces. Today was no exception. "And?"

"When we turned onto Main Street, I had to stomp on the brakes. The place was crawling with police cars."

"A wreck?"

She shook her head. "No. The whole Main Street Park was roped off with yellow tape, but for the life of me, I can't imagine why. When I slowed down and asked the police officer directing traffic what was going on, he said. . ."—Carly tucked her chin and mimicked the deep voice—" 'Official police business, ma'am. Keep moving, please.' So I kept moving. The kids were dyin' for hot fudge sundaes anyway."

"That's weird. Wonder if somebody stole the mayor's car again? Remember a couple of years ago when those three kids took it for a joyride?"

Carly laughed and fished a rubber band out of the little jar on my desk. "Byron was fit to be tied, wasn't he? I saw a clip of an interview with him and Amelia on Channel 8's Web site. The esteemed first lady of Lake View kept saying, 'We've been violated.' But the mayor was literally hopping mad." She twisted the rubber band around her finger.

"His temper is as big as his ego." I stopped short of saying what we both knew. *And both are considerably larger than his brain.*

"Speaking of ego, you know what? Maybe John's dog got off its leash in the park and he used his power as police chief to commandeer the whole department to help him find it."

We've known John since the sandbox, so we never miss an opportunity to give him a hard time about his "powerful" position as police chief of our little town. But Carly's tongue-in-cheek scenario made me think of my early morning chase. "That reminds me. . ."

When I finished the story, she laughed. "I can see you now—holding up that billfold, trying to act normal in front of Brendan."

Ack. "I just remembered I didn't get an answer when I rang the bell at the Templetons' this morning. I meant to call later, but it's been wild here today."

"So you still have his wallet?"

"Sure do. I feel awful. Then again, if he hadn't lost it, I wouldn't have had to run in the rain this morning."

"Well, like I always say, when in doubt, blame a man." She shot me with the rubber band.

"Ouch." I rubbed my arm and tucked the rubber band in my pocket. "Seriously, though—I wish we knew what happened. I may swing by the park on my way home. After that I can drop Hank's wallet off at the *Monitor* and kill two birds with one stone."

"Going by the park won't do you any good. You know you'll get into it with John if he catches you snooping around. Might as well watch the news and save yourself the grief."

Carly had the curiosity of a dishrag sometimes.

"So are the kids adjusting to their new school?"

"They haven't said much." Carly narrowed her eyes. "Why? Have you heard something?"

Now she was curious. Guess it depended on the subject. "No. As far as I know, there haven't been any problems. The girls seem to love it here."

I picked up our family picture from my desk and worried the dust off the oak frame with my finger. Sixteen-year-old Zac towered over his mom and even stood a good four inches above my five-six. How had he grown up so quickly? Suddenly I felt old. "I know Zac didn't want to move, but he seems to be settling in. Is he still enjoying his paper route?"

Carly shrugged. "Who knows? Sugar, I do good to get three words out of him." A rueful grin flitted across her face. "Usually the three are *Mom, I'm hungry*."

"What did I tell you?" I smiled. "Normal teenage boy who happened to get in with the wrong crowd. You worry too much."

"Maybe so. I hate that he has to leave the house while it's still dark. Try the school golf team, I said. But no, he had to have *private* lessons from a pro." Carly held up her hand. "You don't have to remind me. I know I'm the one who told him he'd have to come up with the money on his own. But for goodness' sake, I never dreamed he'd want lessons bad enough to get a job. Especially not one that starts before daylight."

"He loves golf."

"Just like his daddy," Carly said. "Only Zac's got talent. Travis didn't play very well, but he always had to watch those tournaments on TV." She sighed. "I kind of wish Zac didn't remember that."

"You think subconsciously he hopes that if he's good at golf, his dad will see him in some tournament on television and love him enough to come back home?"

Carly arched an eyebrow. "In other words, is he living in a dream world? Don't think I haven't thought about that. The therapist said every time Zac hits a milestone in his life, the rejection issues might start up again. I guess sixteen *is* a milestone."

My stomach clenched the way it always did when I thought about Travis. Running off to California with Miss Stick Figure ten years ago had been more important to the loser than sticking around to help Carly raise their six-year-old son and unborn twins. Okay, so her name wasn't Miss Stick Figure, but that's how I always thought of the anorexic model he'd latched onto—as a caricature, rather than a real person.

"Whatever the reason, golf means a lot to Zac. I probably should have just given him the money for the lessons." Carly's words jarred me back to the present.

"No, he'll appreciate it more in the long run this way. And a job will keep him busy and out of trouble. Remember what Mama always says about idle hands."

Speaking of idle hands, I pulled a rag from my bottom drawer and gave my desktop pictures a hasty dusting. Guilt never loses its power, even when served as leftovers from childhood.

Carly grinned and nodded toward the cloth. "Afraid the devil might be lookin' for a new workshop?"

If only I'd known how busy the devil already was in our sleepy little town, I definitely wouldn't have laughed.

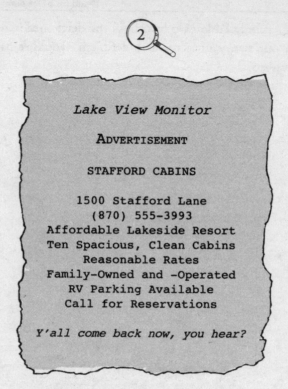

Lake View Monitor

ADVERTISEMENT

STAFFORD CABINS

1500 Stafford Lane
(870) 555-3993
Affordable Lakeside Resort
Ten Spacious, Clean Cabins
Reasonable Rates
Family-Owned and -Operated
RV Parking Available
Call for Reservations

Y'all come back now, you hear?

I should have listened to Carly and skipped the park. The six o'clock news would have given me more information than I'd gotten from John when I tried to climb over the yellow tape. And without the childish name-calling.

"Jen, you're the last person that needs to be here." John gave me his chief-of-police stone-faced glare. "Go home."

Lucky for him, I had it on good authority—his

20

wife, Denise—that he was a softy inside. "You going to arrest me if I don't?" I picked up a gum wrapper near my feet and put it in my pocket. *See what a model citizen I am? I hate litter.*

"This is a serious police matter."

Obviously, somebody's been watching too many cop shows. He's starting to learn the vernacular.

He spun away from me in a classic dismissal technique then must have decided I might not take the hint. He turned back and hiked up the waist of his uniform pants with an air of authority. "You need to go home."

In a minute, he'd be tucking his thumbs in his waistband and patting his spare tire with his fingers. My friend was morphing into the sheriff from *Smokey and the Bandit* before my very eyes. What was with the go-home mantra? "Just tell me what's going on." I nodded to the bright yellow tape stretched around the Bradford pear trees behind him. "Did someone get her purse snatched? Or did you find a dead body in the bushes?"

He ran his hand over his face. "Do you have to be so nosy?"

I didn't answer, and he turned to walk away.

"Fine!" I called to his back. "I've got to return Hank's wallet over at the *Monitor*! Maybe he'll have some answers!"

"What?" John's head snapped around. For the first time he didn't seem in any hurry for me to leave. "Why do you have Hank's wallet?"

I allowed myself a grin. Maybe my funny story would loosen up our esteemed chief. Though it's a well-guarded police secret, he does have a sense of humor. For the third time that day, I recounted the early morning dog chase, leaving out Brendan's appearance. John didn't need to know everything. Or so I thought. Twenty minutes later—after I'd answered a hundred questions ranging from "What time was it when you first saw the dog?" to "Did you see anyone else while you were out?"—I'd changed my mind. And, of course, in answer to the last question, I had to tell John about running into Brendan.

"Why are you asking me so many questions?" I'd patiently answered his. Surely he could answer mine. "Was Hank's billfold stolen?"

John snapped his lips together so definitely that I wouldn't have been surprised if he'd made a locking motion with his fingers by his mouth and pretended to throw away the key. Instead, he frowned. "I can't say right now."

"How convenient."

"You've got the wallet with you?"

I pulled the billfold out of my pocket, and John latched onto it.

"What do you want with it?" I refused to let it go.

"I thought I'd save you some trouble and get it back to its rightful owner." He tugged.

Yeah, right. "You don't want me to talk to Hank." I tugged back.

"Look, Jenna, didn't anybody ever tell you curiosity killed the cat?" He tugged again, but his eyes weren't angry anymore. Instead, something that looked suspiciously like concern clouded his gaze.

That proverb kept cropping up in my life. Maybe it *was* time to go home. I let go of the wallet and left John regaining his balance as I crunched across the leaf-covered parking area to my car. Even the Quik-Mart across the road was overrun with cops. But it was hard to tell if that was because of the store's proximity to the park or the appeal of the best doughnuts in town.

I reached in the driver's window and unlocked the door. Leaving the windows down about four inches probably wasn't very smart at a crime scene, but my cat had to have air.

"You don't think I'm nosy, do you, Neuro?"

She blinked at me from her travel carrier. But she didn't make a sound.

Okay, I admit I waited for a response. Maybe I needed to get out more.

When I pulled into my driveway, I saw Carly relaxing on my porch swing, her feet up on the railing and her red-painted toenails peeking out of her brown leather sandals. The golden retriever lay on the porch next to her, looking way too at home. I tromped up the steps, clutching Neuro's carrier in my hand.

"You went by the park anyway, didn't you?" Carly called.

"Yep."

"And had a fuss with John." It wasn't a question. My sister obviously had no confidence in my diplomatic skills.

I set the carrier down to get my key out of my purse, ignoring Carly's knowing look. "Actually, he was nice enough to take Hank's wallet off my hands and save me the trouble of returning it." The dog trotted over and looked into the carrier, his tail wagging against the wooden porch. Neuro hissed and spat. "But yes, we had words. And I'm pretty sure he had an ulterior motive for taking the billfold, since he interrogated me about how I got it." I slid the key into the lock and maneuvered Neuro inside. "Want to say 'I told you so'?"

"I would, but I'm too hungry." Carly followed me in, and for the second time that day, I shut the door in the dog's face. Inside the house, I released the carrier latch, and Neuro jumped up on the bay window to continue taunting the canine from a safer distance.

"Me, too. What do you want to eat?"

"Do you feel like getting a pizza?" Carly grimaced. "Not that I can afford the points."

"Pizza sounds good." I can't believe she worries about dieting with her curves. Every male in the vicinity stops and stares when she walks by. With my boyish figure, if a man whistles when I'm around, I assume he's calling his dog. But that's life. We always want what we don't have. "Let me get a quick shower and we'll go."

As I twisted my hair up on top of my head and secured it with a bear-claw clip, I had an epiphany. Since I'd come back to Lake View after my meltdown, I'd actually been pretty happy with my life—a family who loved me, a low-pressure job I enjoyed, an undemanding social schedule.

But then came my twenty-eighth birthday. I'm not sure why this insignificant milestone hit me so hard. Maybe I was still dealing with Colton's death. Although I think the counseling had helped me come to grips with that. Or it could have been that, even though Carly had been divorced forever, at least she had three wonderful kids, and they were her world. I was on a waxed slide to thirty with no hint of romance in sight.

To celebrate that particular birthday, Carly and the kids had come up from Atlanta for the weekend. Mama babysat while Carly and I stayed up half the night at my place, watching an Elvis movie marathon. As the *Love Me Tender* credits rolled, I confessed I was afraid I'd grow old alone. Then she blew me away with a confession of her own. She thought Travis's defection had given me a deep-seated lack of trust in the male race. Yep. She accused me to my face of sabotaging my own relationships because of my reluctance to commit.

I'm not sure how it happened, but by the time the sun came up, I had committed to a deadline. Find Mr. Right or, as I told Carly, Mr. As Good as It Gets by my thirtieth birthday. Or at least make a serious effort.

And even though I'm the first to admit I have commitment issues, I've tried. I honestly have. As the hot water showered down on me, I ran through the list of possible candidates one more time.

One man I went out with made a pass at the waitress

before we even ordered. And I'll never forget the cop who leaned over to me in the middle of the movie and said, "So I guess if we start dating, I can work out at the club for free?" Then there was a guy from our singles' group at church who brought over an *X-Files* DVD for us to watch. I actually enjoyed the episode, but after it was over, he showed me passages in the Bible that he claimed proved Jesus died for aliens, too.

The list could go on. Unfortunately. Which led me to Brendan Stiles. Maybe my date with him tomorrow night would be better than I expected. A girl could hope. It had been almost two years since that night I set the deadline with Carly as my witness. My big 3-0 was less than four months away.

After my shower, I found Carly sitting in the living room, flipping through the channels. Neuro amused herself by scratching at the pile of clean blankets. I picked up a quilt and tossed one end to Carly. "Make yourself useful."

"Thanks. I never get to fold laundry." She stood and took the proffered corners and joined me in a ritual we'd performed together since elementary school. Mama had taught us simple steps to accompany the chore of folding towels and sheets, as well as quilts and blankets. Between our own house and the ten cabins we rented out, there'd been plenty of work to keep us busy.

"Remember how Mama always made work a game?" Carly seemed to read my mind.

"Yes." I'd helped with the cabins, but my swim training had come first. The bulk of the work had fallen to Carly.

"She doesn't understand why I can't do the same thing with the twins and Zac." Carly slammed a folded quilt onto the pile. "Maybe now since we're living with her, she'll see it's not as easy to teach kids things these days."

For Carly, that constituted a tirade. I didn't know what to say.

She flopped back onto the couch. "I guess that sounded ungrateful, didn't it? I'm thankful Mama and Daddy let us move in with them. And goodness knows, I need the job helping out with the cabins. But Zac is like a stranger these days, and for the life of me, I can't figure out what's happened to my precious little twins. . . ."

"I know." The twins had gone from being as close as two pieces of gum in the same wrapper to elevating sibling rivalry to an art form. And as for Zac, well, teenagers are hard to figure out. I'd learned that first-hand when I taught PE and coached. Anything could happen. I shuddered. Anything at all.

My phone on the end table rang. With the instinct of a mother whose children are not with her, Carly glanced at the caller ID.

She groaned. "Oh no. I bet the twins are at it again."

I nodded for her to answer the phone.

"Hi, Mama. The girls drivin' you nuts?" Carly held the handset between her ear and her shoulder and picked up a quilt to fold.

All the color left her face. She slammed the phone

down and shot to her feet, dropping the quilt as if it burned her hands.

I grabbed her arm. "What's wrong? What did Mama say?"

"The police." She jerked away from me and snatched her keys from the table.

"What about the police?" Carly's legs are shorter, but I found myself running to keep up with her as she darted down the hallway to the door.

"Zac."

Was I going to have to shake the facts out of her? "Carly, talk to me here. What do the police have to do with Zac? Is he in trouble?"

"I don't know. Oh my goodness." Tears streamed down her face.

As we reached the car, I gently pried the keys from her fingers. "I'll drive."

She nodded. "It's Hank Templeton. They found his body in the park."

I clapped my hand to my mouth. "His wallet."

Carly sobbed. "He's been murdered. They want to question Zac."

My mind raced as we flew down the road to our parents' house. My sixteen-year-old nephew couldn't hurt someone if his life depended on it. But surely no one in Lake View was capable of murder. Some vagrant must have stumbled into our safe little town, decided to lift Hank's wallet, and had gotten carried away. We all knew the editor and owner of the *Lake View Monitor* walked home from the newspaper office every night through the park. Maybe he'd surprised some bum on a bench. Knowing Hank, he probably shook him awake and demanded he stop loitering. But still my heart ached that the grouchy old man was dead.

Had the dog gotten the wallet from the murderer? Or from Hank's body in the park? The park. The mystery of the park's yellow tape was solved, but why question Zac? A paperboy. "Wait a minute, Carly. If Hank's been murdered, it's only natural they'd want to talk to his employees, right?"

She looked at me as if I had two heads. "You think that's it? That they're talking to all the people who work at the newspaper?"

"I'm sure of it."

She sank back against the seat and covered her face with her hands. "I was afraid that they'd found out about Atlanta."

I eased the car into the Stafford Cabins entryway and gasped. A black-and-white patrol car sat in the driveway. Flashing blue lights imprinted the surreal scene in my mind as two police officers started toward us. Ed and Seth, just a couple of locals with badges. Seth I knew especially well since he was the cop who'd gone out with me, hoping to get a free membership to the health club. Still, we hadn't ended on bad terms. Surely they didn't need blue lights to ask Zac some questions.

Daddy stood with his arm around Mama, and the twins huddled against them.

I squeezed Carly's arm. "Don't think the worst. Let's just pray."

Carly peeked between her fingers. "Oh Lord, please help us. Hasn't Zac been through enough? Haven't we all?"

I breathed a prayer of my own as Zac pulled in right behind us.

The policemen marched past us to Zac's jeep. Carly and I erupted out of her car in time to hear Ed ask Zac to step out of the vehicle.

"We need to ask you some questions about your relationship with Hank Templeton."

"Like what?" Zac's voice shook, but he stepped out onto the gravel. My heart thudded against my rib cage as we followed the officers up to the porch.

"Hank's been murdered," Carly blurted, then gasped as Ed gave her a hard glare.

"Son, where were you this morning around four thirty?" he asked.

"He was at work." Carly's voice cracked.

Ed glared at her again, and an ashen-faced Zac looked at the ground. Flash back to an adorable four-year-old ducking his head when his mom asked if he'd put crayons in the VCR. This was so not good. I knew Zac didn't kill Hank, but he looked so guilty.

"Is that true?" Ed kept his gaze on Zac.

Zac slowly shook his head. "I was just drivin' around town."

Carly dug her fingernails into my arm. "Zac?" She sounded like she'd been sucking helium. "What about your paper route?"

"Hank fired me three days ago, Mom. I'm sorry."

My nephew, who hadn't even cried when he broke his collarbone, swiped tears from his cheeks.

Carly put her hand over her mouth, but her eyes screamed.

Ed frowned. "So let me get this straight. You didn't have a job anymore, but you still left home before daylight?"

As if we were all attached at the neck by a wire, our heads swiveled toward Zac. *Please let him have a good explanation.*

"I figured Mr. Templeton might get over it in a few days and let me come back to work; then I wouldn't hafta tell my mom."

As dumb as that sounded, I'm sure it made perfect sense to a sixteen-year-old. He'd probably thought Carly would make him quit his golf lessons.

"Witnesses say you had a loud argument with Mr. Templeton when he fired you. Is that true?" Seth shot me an apologetic glance. In spite of our one disastrous date, he practically lived at the club. And paid his own way. Zac nodded.

"I'm afraid you're going to have to go downtown with us to answer some more questions." Officer Ed Arnett looked like he'd rather be in the dentist chair than on Mama and Daddy's front porch. He turned to Carly. "You'll have to come, too, since he's a minor."

Carly staggered as if an invisible force had slammed into her. I reached out to steady her, trying to ignore my own trembling legs. Mama put her arms protectively around her granddaughters. "Girls, let's go in the house."

As Hayley and Rachel reluctantly obeyed, I drew

strength from the normalcy in Mama's voice, even though I knew it was forced. If only Carly and I, and especially Zac, were young enough to "go in the house" with Mama, instead of facing the harsh reality on the porch.

Even at sixty, Daddy stood tall and straight beside Zac and Carly. As a boy, he'd been a swimmer—an Olympic hopeful until he'd torn his rotator cuff in a sandlot baseball game. When we were growing up, he was a deputy sheriff, and though those days were long gone, he still carried himself with the air of a humble president—in control but not arrogant. "Now, Ed, listen here. Zac's not going anywhere without me. I'll take him and his mom to the station, and you boys can follow us."

Ed, the grizzled-before-his-time veteran cop, didn't seem to mind a bit that his old Little League coach had just referred to him as a "boy." Instead, he nodded and glanced at his young partner. "Seth? What do you think?"

"Sure, that'd be okay."

As ridiculous as this was, if I kept telling myself that the police officers were only doing their job, maybe I could keep from slugging them.

Daddy turned to me and pushed an errant strand of hair behind my ear. "Stay with your mama and the girls, honey. We'll talk to John and get this worked out and call you when we know anything."

Unlike Carly, who had butted heads with our parents on a regular basis right up until she ran off with

Travis on the night of her high school graduation, I'd rarely ever disagreed with Mama or Daddy. But this was the exception. I belonged with Carly and Zac. "I'll help Mama get the girls settled and then meet y'all at the station."

His eyes widened, and I lifted my chin.

Without a word, he nodded then shepherded Carly and Zac into his crew cab truck.

> ### *Lake View Monitor*
>
> #### *MONITOR* MOURNS EDITOR
>
> The body of *Lake View Monitor* editor and owner Hank Templeton was discovered early Friday morning in Main Street Park, the victim of an apparent homicide. The local police department is withholding details pending an investigation. . . .

Twenty minutes later, I rushed into the Lake View police station. Before I could ask the uniformed desk clerk for information, I spotted Carly slumped on a bench.

The haunted look in her eyes took me back to the days right after Travis left. Ten years of healing down the tubes.

"Daddy wouldn't allow them to question Zac without a lawyer, but they'd only let one of us stay with him until the attorney gets here." She shrugged. "I told him to do it. He's a rock." She nodded down at the twisted Kleenex in her hands. "I'm a basket case."

I sank onto the wooden bench and put my arm around her shoulders. "Why don't I call Denise?" Sometimes John's wife was the only one who could get the hard-line chief of police to see reason.

Carly shook her head. "Daddy talked to John when we first got here. John said he wished there was something he could do, but there's not. He can't afford to do us any special favors. Especially in a high-profile case like this."

Hank Templeton. Married into one of the wealthiest families in Lake View. And although they despised each other, he and Mayor Byron Stanton, who had married into the same family, had been brothers-in-law.

John and his department would be under tremendous pressure to solve this case. But surely they wouldn't railroad an innocent sixteen-year-old. "So you called a lawyer?"

Carly nodded. "Daddy thought we should get Alex Campbell since he's back in town." She looked up at me. "Are you okay with that?"

I could almost hear the rusty hinges on the corner of my heart where I'd stashed all my unresolved feelings for Alex Campbell. I gave the door a mental shove and was gratified to hear it clink shut once more. "Sure. I'm fine with it."

Alex's dad had been my swim coach from the time I was eight. Alex was two years older, but he let me tag along after him. Until I turned fourteen and he started tagging after me.

Alex and swimming. My two youthful obsessions.

Both lost the summer before I turned seventeen. When I slunk home from the Olympics in need of a friend, Alex left for college, and since his parents moved away shortly after, he'd never returned.

Until now.

A door across the hall opened. John stepped out and, studiously ignoring me, motioned to Carly. Maybe I'd gone too far at the park today. But so had he! Tricking me into giving him Hank's wallet. "Carly, I think you need to come on in here with your dad and Zac, after all."

I stood with Carly and gave her a hug. "I'll be out here praying for y'all," I whispered.

"Thanks." Carly hurried into the room.

"John, can I talk to you for a minute?"

He turned around and glared at me. "Don't you think we've talked enough today, Jen?"

"Aw, c'mon, John. You know I don't think you're power-hungry. And among other things, you called me a busybody!" My anger flared. "Plus, you basically lied to me about Hank's wallet! But you don't see me pouting. This is my nephew we're talking about." John and I had bickered all through school. Even though he's married now and the well-respected chief of police, we still argued like five-year-olds. But this was serious.

"Look, Jenna, it's been a long day for all of us. I'm worried about Zac, too. But the best thing you can do for him now is let the police handle it." He hurried down the hall before I could protest.

Alone on the bench, I murmured a prayer then

flipped open my cell phone and called Mama. I couldn't imagine being at home with no way of knowing what was going on.

"Mama?"

"Jen!" She lowered her voice. "What's happened?"

"Carly and Daddy are in a room with Zac. They're waiting for Alex Campbell. Daddy called him."

"Oh, good." I could hear the relief in Mama's tone. Alex still inspired confidence in people, even after all these years.

Daddy had been drinking coffee at the Lake View Diner with the same bunch of men every weekday morning for the last twenty years. It usually took a year or two for a newcomer to break into the group, but when Alex had come back to town recently to hang out his shingle, he'd been accepted immediately into their early morning circle.

"Yes, Alex will no doubt save the day." I regretted the sarcasm as soon as it left my lips. But not nearly as much as I did when I heard a masculine cough beside me.

"Thanks for the vote of confidence."

As I looked up into his gorgeous blue eyes, I barely remembered saying good-bye to Mama.

After hearing about it for a month, I was seeing it for myself. Alex Campbell had, indeed, come home.

Early Saturday morning, I popped open a tube of crescent rolls as Carly stumbled, bleary-eyed, into the kitchen. I felt a little guilty thinking about food at a time like this, but we didn't ever get that pizza, and my sandwich from lunch yesterday was long gone.

"Hey. Did you get any sleep?"

"A little bit. Mama insisted I take something." Carly grimaced. "I'm sorry you couldn't."

Right after my granddad's death several years ago, Mama had given us each a sleeping pill. Carly had slept like a log, but I'd bounced off the walls all night, finally falling asleep in the middle of the funeral. Then it took forever for them to wake me up. No matter what the disaster now, no one in my family would ever offer me another sleeping pill.

Carly shrugged. "Actually, not sleeping was probably a blessing. At least you didn't have any bad dreams." She pulled a mug off the shelf and padded over to the coffee-pot. "I appreciate your staying here all night and helping get the kids to bed. After Alex got there and they started questioning Zac, I figured Mama needed you more than we did."

"Yep. Holding down that wooden bench didn't seem all that important." No need to mention that once Alex arrived, I'd practically run out of the station. "Speaking of Zac. . ." I pushed the creamer toward her then put the rolls in the oven and set the timer. "How's he taking all this?"

"Like anybody would, I guess. He feels guilty for not telling me about getting fired, but he can't believe the police would think he might be a murderer. Ah, Jen, he's terrified." Carly perched on a bar stool. "And

I'll tell you, so am I." She put her head in her hands.

My heart wrenched. "I know. I am, too."

Carly looked up, tears sliding down her cheeks. "But regardless of Zac's *record*, you know he wouldn't hurt a flea."

"Of course I do. But we know him." We'd known he actually *was* holding a package for a friend when the police found drugs in his locker in Atlanta. Carly had started making plans to move back to Lake View shortly after the incident.

Carly grimaced. "And the police don't."

I handed her a Kleenex. "I didn't get a chance to ask you last night, with everyone so wiped out. Why'd Hank fire Zac?"

"Tuesday morning that old wreck Zac calls a car wouldn't start, and he had to give it a boost off my battery. He never even woke me up. My baby's growin' up so fast." She sniffed and wiped her eyes. "Anyway, when he finally got to work, Hank lit into him for being late. Zac told him about the car, but Hank still didn't let up."

I felt a surge of irritation at Hank, but then I remembered he was dead and immediately felt guilty. "Hank always could be hard to take. Remember how he used to yell at us if Beauty ever went to the bathroom in the edge of his yard when we were walking her?"

"Yeah, well, unfortunately, with half of the newspaper staff there, Hank fired him, and Zac yelled that he'd be sorry."

"Oh no." I sank onto the stool beside her. "No wonder the police are questioning him. Did you ask him what he meant?"

Carly nodded. "He said he was thinking about how many of the other delivery people were slackers and how he had been trying so hard to do it right." As she spoke, tears spilled down her cheeks again. "So he meant that Hank was losing someone who cared about doing a good job. He thought Hank would be sorry when he realized it."

"I can see that."

"I can see it, too, but it sounds bad, doesn't it?"

"Yeah." I knew Carly didn't want false words of reassurance. Maybe it was time to change the subject. "So did Alex handle things okay?" Heat rushed to my cheeks as I remembered his overhearing me talking to Mama last night. The perfect ending to the perfect day. Not.

"Yes." She wiped her eyes and glanced at me. "Are you sure you don't have a problem with Alex being Zac's lawyer?"

"I'm sure. Why should I?"

"Why should you? Sugar, this is me you're talking to. Remember? That torch you carried for him made the Olympic torch look like a little birthday candle. And it broke my heart, too, when he left town that summer without sayin' good-bye to you."

Actually, he had called, but I'd refused to talk to him. The agony of my defeat was still too fresh. I was seventeen. Who knew he'd never call again?

"Anyway, he said it was good to see you and asked what you were doing these days."

"Really?" I grimaced at my high-pitched tone. I took a sip of my coffee and tried to sound casual. "Strange we haven't seen him at church."

"He's been closing out his old office on the weekends. Had to go again today, actually. But he'll be at church tomorrow."

"That's nice. So what did you tell him?" I picked an imaginary fleck from my Eeyore pajama bottoms. "About me, I mean."

"Oh, not much. I'm pretty sure Daddy had already bragged up your job at the health club and made you sound like a partner." She frowned. "Which you should be. At the very least. So I told him you were seeing Brendan."

I flinched.

"Was I wrong?" Carly raised an eyebrow.

I shrugged. "Not really. I canceled for tonight, though." The oven timer went off, and I pulled the rolls out. "Can you grab the butter and jelly?"

"Sure." Carly retrieved them from the refrigerator and put them next to the basket of hot rolls. "Anyway, for the life of me, I don't know what we would have done without Alex. He believed Zac about last year's trouble."

"Sounds like he has good judgment." Although, surely, if he'd had very good judgment, he'd never have stayed away from Lake View for so long. I pushed a buttered roll toward Carly. Enough about Alex.

"Thanks." She cradled the hot bread in both hands. "I'm not counting points today."

"I noticed you set out the real butter." That detail, more than anything, made me realize the extreme level of her stress.

"Sometimes you have to have the real thing." She squeezed a big glob of strawberry jelly onto the roll and took a bite.

"Zac still asleep?"

"Probably. Bless his heart, he was worn out. I guess Mama and Daddy went out to breakfast this morning?" She looked around the kitchen as if expecting our parents to pop out of the cabinets. "I told them last night, the more normal we can keep things, the better."

Our parents rarely splurged, but their Saturday breakfasts out were a time for them to talk over the week. They sure had a lot to talk about this morning. "Do you think the police will question Zac again?"

"I don't know." Carly finished off her coffee. "They told him not to leave town." She wiped her hands on her napkin. "For the life of me, I can't imagine why they took Zac in. A lot of people had run-ins with Hank. You know what? On the way home, Zac told us that even his golf teacher had a fight with Hank recently."

"Do the police know that?" I felt a little guilty, hoping to incriminate someone else, but *someone* murdered Hank, and it wasn't Zac.

"Don't you dare tell them!" We spun around to

see Zac standing in the doorway, his eyes red-rimmed. "Elliott didn't kill Hank!"

"I'm sure he didn't." Carly's quiet tone couldn't hide her frustration. "But neither did you."

"Mom, Elliott got mad at Hank over something you might understand. His fiancée left him."

"What did that have to do with Hank?" I asked casually, my heart in my throat. Had Hank been cheating on Marge and been killed by a jealous boyfriend?

"Not Hank, the paper. It had something to do with the paper. I don't know what." Zac stomped over to the refrigerator and snagged a single-serving bottle of orange juice. He glared at his mom as he popped the top. "I'm sorry I even told you. He was only trying to make me feel better about getting fired."

"I understand, son, but—" Carly cast me a pleading glance.

"Want a crescent roll?" When in doubt, distract.

Sure enough, Zac nodded and took one. Another dangerous situation defused with food. "I'm going out to the course."

"Today?" Carly looked dumbfounded.

Zac grunted. "I'm a suspect, not a prisoner." He snatched one more roll and blew out like a spring tornado.

We sat in silence for a few seconds; then Carly swiveled her bar stool back and forth. "You know, I can't help but wonder. . ."

"What?"

"Well, we know Zac didn't kill Hank. And Zac's positive Elliott didn't. So who did?"

"Good question. I've been thinking the same thing." I picked up Carly's dishes. "They always say it's most likely a family member. But somehow I can't imagine Marge killing anyone." Like an eccentric old aunt, Marge had been around as long as I could remember, giving us gum after church when we were little and buying chocolate bars and Girl Scout cookies from us as we grew older. Her sister, Amelia, relished her high-profile role as the mayor's wife, but Marge had seemed content in her middle-class life with cantankerous old Hank.

"Oh, I don't know." An impish grin flitted across Carly's tired face. "Maybe she finally managed to nag him to death," she drawled.

"Carly Elizabeth Reece! You are so bad."

"I was kidding." Her smile disappeared. "But I shouldn't have said it. It's hard enough to get along with a normal man. Marge deserves a badge of honor for putting up with Hank's bad temper and know-it-all attitude for so many years."

"Well, we've known her forever. I can't believe she killed him, so who does that leave?" I wrung out the dishcloth and wiped off the counter.

"You're the one who's always got your nose in those murder mysteries. You tell me."

I rolled my eyes. "Oh yes, that makes me an expert." I tossed the cloth into the sink. "Seriously, though—if we could find out who did it, that would clear Zac."

"We? You got a frog in your pocket?" Carly's voice

squeaked, and she shook her head. "I get scared readin' those books. I'm not about to live one."

"Not even for Zac?" Yes, that was below the belt, but if I was going to get to the bottom of this, I had to have help.

Carly shook her head again. "The best thing we can do for Zac is pray and let the police do their job. They'll find the killer, and that'll prove Zac's innocence."

Where had I heard that before? Was Carly the mouthpiece for the chief of police now? "I know. You're right, and we *will* pray. But they say God helps those who help themselves, so—"

"Oh, Jen, that's not even in the Bible. Besides, this is too important for us to play detective. We don't want to make things worse for Zac." Carly hesitated. "Sugar, your track record's not that great. Remember in school how mixed up things would get every time you decided to 'help' figure things out?"

I bristled. "I've helped plenty of people."

Carly's smile was gentle. "Like Susan?"

"How was I supposed to know that girl with Barry was his cousin? They were picking out jewelry together."

"Yeah, gifts for the groomsmen."

"Once I cleared up the misunderstanding, they got back together." They'd even been able to get the same date and time for the ceremony. All I'd really done was inject a little excitement into their post-engagement/pre-wedding lull.

"And marked you off the invitation list."

Some people. One little mistake and they never let

you live it down. I shrugged. "This is different. What can it hurt if we do a little innocent snooping?"

"What can it *hurt*?" Carly's animated face was such a contrast to her earlier tears that it was almost worth the disagreement. "Are you kidding? This isn't a game or some high school prank. You're talkin' about goin' after a cold-blooded killer."

Lake View Monitor

OBITUARY

Respected editor and owner of the *Lake View Monitor*, Henry (Hank) Theodore Templeton died Friday morning. (See front-page story for details.)

Templeton is survived by his beloved wife, Margaret Smith Templeton; one son, Henry Theodore Templeton Jr., currently in Europe; two sisters, Elisen Bradenburg of Arizona and Lilly Jordan of Missouri; and numerous nieces and nephews.

Templeton was a member of the local VFW, the Lake View Zoning Committee, and the Lake View Chamber of Commerce. Funeral arrangements are incomplete.

Green bean casserole and marshmallow salad. Haute cuisine for dummies. Normally this would have been the perfect opportunity for Carly to display her culinary skills. Cooking actually helped her to relieve stress, but she was exhausted, so Mama and I opted for quick and easy.

Poor Marge. How would she react to Zac's being a suspect in her husband's murder? I was in no hurry to find out. If Mama hadn't played the Christian-duty card, I wouldn't be standing here this fine Saturday afternoon, ringing the Templetons' doorbell.

Marge's best friend, Lois, opened the door. "Thanks for coming by." Her hushed tone matched her somber face. I suppose with her being the town librarian, *whisper* is her native language.

"How's Marge?" Mama asked.

Lois shook her head. "I think she's still in shock."

We nodded and followed her through the standing-room-only crowd. Everyone from church and the neighborhood had turned out to pay their respects to Hank's widow. In the South we show our sympathy with food offerings, and judging by the number of steaming dishes filling the table, everyone in Lake View felt sorry for Marge.

We squeezed our own offerings into the sea of casseroles. Lois would have her hands full after the funeral, helping Marge discreetly dispose of the leftovers.

"You ladies come in and have a seat." Lois gestured toward the living room. When we stepped in, it was as if someone had hit the MUTE button. We nodded politely into the silence.

The news of Zac's trip downtown had definitely made its way around the local grapevine. Mama always said, "Good news travels fast, but bad news travels faster," and she was right again.

A low-hum chorus of greetings floated in our direction; then mercifully, everyone went back to their quiet conversations. Lois motioned toward the chintz couch, and the gray-haired Llewellen sisters scooted closer together to make room for us. After we settled in, Lois perched on the arm of Marge's overstuffed chair and patted her on the back. "Is there anything I can get for you?" She reminded me of an anxious lady-in-waiting.

"No, thanks. I'm fine." Marge smiled at us. "Elizabeth. Jenna. It's good to see you. Theo's on his way, Jenna. I know he'll want to see you." Marge's eyes were red and swollen, but her abnormally high-pitched voice and pseudo-perky attitude suggested that the doctor had probably given her some pills to lessen the shock.

"Marge, we're so sorry to hear about Hank's death. Lake View won't be the same without him."

That was true. Mama always knew the right thing to say. If it had been left up to me, I probably wouldn't have mentioned Hank. And if I had—well, let's just say it's a good thing I let Mama do the talking.

Marge beamed. "Hank loved Lake View. The newspaper was his life." Her smile froze then melted into a frown. "Amelia used to say he should have married the *Monitor* instead of me."

Now there's a thought. Since the wife is the most likely suspect, maybe the Monitor *killed him.*

Valium was probably responsible for this emotional roller coaster, but the wistful tone in her voice clutched at my heart. Hank had been a pain, but he'd been *her* pain.

"Amelia. *Humph*," Lois muttered, looking like she'd taken a drink of curdled milk.

Mama leaned forward and patted Marge's hand. "Hank was lucky to have you, Marge. He loved you very much."

Suddenly, Marge plopped back against the chair. "He had a funny way of showing it sometimes." Tears spilled onto her cheeks.

A million questions flooded my mind, and I barely stopped them before they tumbled out of my mouth. Had Hank been abusive? Something beyond your garden-variety crankiness? I settled for a hopefully leading, "Oh?"

Mama glared at me, and I could see she knew I was trying to launch a little investigation of my own. How do mothers do that?

"Hank did love you, Marge," Lois said soothingly.

"Yes, I'm sure he did, but you know as well as I do, by the time the bridge club meets Monday, they'll be wondering if I murdered him." Marge squeaked on the last word.

The Llewellen sisters gasped, and even Mama looked a little nonplussed. This visit had suddenly gone from obligatory to interesting.

"No, they won't!" Mama and Lois chorused.

I opened my mouth to gently ask why they would think that, but before I could speak, Marge burst out, "Oh yes, they will." Her gaze darted from side to side, and she lowered her voice to a conspiratorial whisper. "You know how people talk." She nodded to Mama. "Look at how the news spread about Zac being arrested."

"He wasn't actually arrest—," Mama started.

"Can you believe they took that poor child down to the police station? Isn't that the most ridiculous thing you've ever heard? Why, they even came around here asking *me* all kinds of questions. Why didn't I call and report Hank missing?" She shook her head, and her tight curls sprang back and forth. "Why would I call? I never know what time Hank's going to get home. Everybody knows how late he works when he's got his mind on a story. Besides, Lois had one of those twenty-four-hour bugs. I couldn't leave her alone, so I stayed with her. I never dreamed he didn't come home. Isn't that right, Lois?"

Lois nodded, but for a second, I thought I saw a warning expression in her eyes.

Marge looked back to us. "You tell that sweet boy not to worry. I know he didn't kill Hank."

"It's kind of you to be concerned about Zac, Marge," Mama said. "He had a rough night last night, and so did his mother. We'd better get home and check on them." Mama stood, and I quickly did the same. My mother could always be counted on to extricate us gracefully from an awkward social situation. And situations didn't get much more awkward than this.

Marge pushed to her feet and hugged me. The familiar smells of spearmint gum and perm solution transported me back to childhood. Marge was odd, but she deserved to know who killed her husband. And if I had my way, she would.

The doorbell rang. Marge gave Mama a hug and excused herself to answer it.

Mama squeezed Lois's hand. "I'm glad you're here with her."

"Thank you. She'd do the same for me." Her solemn gaze flickered to include me.

I nodded. "Have they made any arrangements yet?"

"Poor Marge." Lois dabbed her eyes with a tissue. "The. . ." She cleared her throat and glanced toward the foyer, where a weeping Marge was enfolded in the rather large embrace of the church secretary. "The authorities say the body won't be released for at least two weeks. Marge doesn't think it's fair to Hank's memory to wait."

"Bless her heart." Mama's voice was soft with sympathy.

"Yes," Lois said. "She's scheduled a memorial service for him at the church Monday afternoon. They'll put a special notice in Sunday's paper."

We hugged Lois and patted Marge's heaving back one more time on the way out the door. When the latch clicked behind us, I glanced at my mother. "You did good, Mama. I felt sorry for Marge, but the air in there was too thick with weirdness."

She frowned. "Marge has always been a little. . .hmm . . .unusual, especially the last year or so, but today was strange, even for her. Poor thing. Even if she was under his thumb all those years, Hank's death has to be hard on her."

"I know. I wish there were more we could do."

"We can visit her whether we enjoy her company right now or not."

If I'd said that, I'd have sounded like Pollyanna, but Mama just sounded gracious.

I reached in my pocket for the keys. "Yeah, but there might be something else we could do, too." Maybe if I led up to this slowly, I could slide under the Mama-meter.

"What do you mean?"

"I don't know. We know a lot of people. Don't you think if we tried, we might figure out what happened to Hank?"

Mama groaned as she walked around to the passenger side. "Jenna, honey. . ."

"Don't worry, Carly's already given me that speech about minding my own business. You don't have to." That is one disadvantage to having a big sister. I hear every for-your-own-good talk twice.

"Why do I get the feeling you didn't listen to her, either?"

I slid into the driver's seat and chose not to answer. As I turned the key, a black car rounded the corner. "Talk about the consummate politician. I never dreamed he would show up here." I nodded toward the Mercedes that was the trademark of Lake View mayor Byron Stanton.

I should have known, though. The mayor was bound to be happy that Hank's scathing editorials were a thing of the past, but he'd squeeze out a few tears for the public's benefit, his classically handsome face twisted into a mournful expression.

Mama nodded. "Looks like he even coaxed Amelia into coming with him. She and Marge haven't spoken in years," she said. "I wonder if they will today."

I braked. "Want to go back and watch?" I nearly laughed aloud at the look of distaste on her face. "Mama, I'm kidding!"

"I know you are. It's just always bothered me that two sisters who were as close as Marge and Amelia used to be could let their husbands pull them apart. Marge needs her sister's support at a time like this. Maybe they can mend fences."

"Maybe so." I thought of the last few editorials Hank had written. "But you know how when somebody dies, there's a tendency to canonize them. Marge may take up the torch and continue the 'Lord Byron' editorials."

"Let's hope not. I agree Byron *is* egotistical, but Hank ran that into the ground. I'm sure our mayor was sick to death of it."

I glanced quickly at Mama. "Sick to death, huh? Interesting choice of words."

The solemn music drifted into the foyer as Carly and I entered the church building. Carly kept her gaze fixed on the faded gold and maroon carpet and stepped back for me to take the lead. She'd tried to beg off, claiming that people would think it was in poor taste for her to attend the memorial service on account of her son's being a suspect, but I wasn't about to come by myself. And I wasn't about to miss it.

"Why did I let you talk me into this?" Carly muttered into my shoulder blades.

I knew the answer to that one but kept my mouth shut. She owed me big-time after the Pampered Chef party I'd endured for her a couple of weeks ago.

I signed our names in the guest book, and we walked to the back row, where three aisle seats were empty.

Carly slid into the inside seat with a low growl. "Honestly, I think I should just go home."

"Relax, it'll be fine."

"Sure it will be. But staying at home with a good book would have been *much* finer," Carly snapped.

I lowered my voice to a soft whisper. "You know, they say the best place to find a murderer is at the victim's funeral."

"But we're not interested in finding a murderer." Her voice rose on the last word.

"Shh. Yes, we are." I turned back toward the front. "Look."

"What?" She followed my gaze and spotted Brendan offering his condolences to Marge. "Brendan? What's he doing here?"

"I have no idea." He hugged Marge then leaned down to embrace Lois, who was sitting next to her bereaved friend.

"Maybe he's a friend of the family."

"Are you ever going to go out with him again?"

"Someday," I said without looking up from the program the funeral director had handed me as we entered, "when there's not so much going on."

"Yeah." Carly sighed. "Surely Zac will be cleared soon. The idea of him murdering someone is ridiculous. And the idea of us attending the victim's funeral is even more ridiculous."

I stuck the program into Carly's black satchel. "If we find the killer, Zac'll be cleared."

"Jenna, we are not—"

"I know we're not officially investigating, but if we pick up a little clue here or there that would exonerate Zac, what can it hurt?"

"That's it. I'm leaving." Carly started to rise, but I put my hand on her arm.

"Wait. Look."

A short, trim man in a dark suit and a red and yellow floral tie walked past us. The well-preserved blond on his arm was decked out in designer black down to her stiletto heels.

"Yeah. Byron and Amelia. So what?" Carly pulled her arm away from me. "They *are* Hank's sister-in-law and brother-in-law. It seems natural to me they would be here."

"Does his million-dollar smile look strained to you? A little stiff? Hers, too, for that matter?"

"Why, yes. Now that you mention it, I wouldn't give you but a hundred thousand for it today," Carly drawled.

"I'm serious," I said.

"Me, too. Have you ever read that Nancy Drew mystery where Nancy suspects everyone and ends up looking like an idiot?"

"No." I turned my attention back to the mayor. He was greeting people as if this were a parade and he and his wife the only float.

"Me, either, but I'm sure there is one."

I rolled my eyes. "If you'd help me look around instead of wasting time wishing you weren't here, we might learn something."

Carly sighed and stared straight ahead.

Shoulder to shoulder, people filled the pews, and the last few aisles, including the one we sat in, consisted of mostly occupied white folding chairs.

I methodically scanned each row, spotting Don Samuels, the butcher from Piggly Wiggly. Two rows down, Angelo Petronelli, from Petronelli Bakery, sat with his family. *The butcher, the baker—all we need now is the candlestick maker.* Immediately Chrysalis Summer, owner of that little bead and candle shop on Main Street, passed in front of my view. Now everyone was accounted for at the funeral of one of Lake View's most prominent citizens.

The newspaper employees were all seated in one section, along with their families. Something about the slumped figure with a blond buzz cut caught my eye.

"Car!" I hissed.

She glanced at me. "What?"

"Does the back of that head look familiar to you?"

I pointed discreetly, covering my finger with my hand. "Right there, on the other side, four rows up," I whispered.

Carly clutched my hand. "It's Zac."

I winced and pried her death grip loose. I nodded, but my mind was spinning. Why would Zac be here? Why hadn't he told us he was coming? He was supposed to be in school. "Who's that sitting by him?"

"It looks like Elliott, his golf instructor." The hurt fled from Carly's face, replaced by determination. "I'm going to go talk to Zac."

"Wait a minute," I said. Making a scene at the funeral wouldn't be a good thing for Zac, and Carly's taut face had *scene* written all over it. "Let's think about this. If he didn't mention he was coming, he probably didn't want you to know. Did you tell him you were going to be here?"

She shook her head.

"Don't you think home would be a better place to discuss it with him? Or at least wait until after the service?"

She nodded and sat back, biting her lip.

"Excuse me, ladies."

I jerked around to meet Alex Campbell's intent gaze. He seemed to be making a habit of sneaking up on me.

"May I sit here?" he whispered.

I nodded dumbly. Carly slid into the vacant seat farther into the row, and I automatically followed suit.

Alex leaned over toward me. "Hey, water girl.

How's life in the deep end?" His standard greeting to me as long as I can remember.

"I'm not so crazy about being in over my head anymore," I whispered, my pulse pounding as loud as my words.

Thankfully, before I had to tread any more dangerous water, Brother Johnson stood and approached the podium. The music and muted conversation stopped.

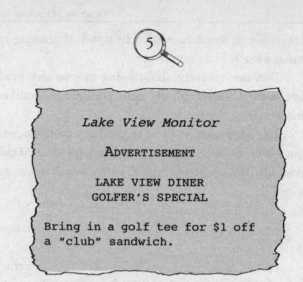

I admired the preacher who could make heavy-handed Hank sound like a candidate for sainthood. But I was glad for Marge's sake that he could come up with comforting words. Theo, Hank's son, had barely made it home in time for the funeral, but he seemed to be holding up very well. Since there was no casket, after the closing prayer, we stood respectfully while Hank's family filed out. What a shame Amelia wasn't close enough to her sister to comfort her at a time like this.

Once we were all outside, I hugged Marge, then Theo.

"Jenna, it's so good to see you."

"You, too, Theo. I'm just sorry about the circumstances." We hugged again, and he took his mom to speak to someone else.

I turned around to find Carly and Alex standing behind me.

"Would you ladies like to get a bite to eat?" Alex lowered his voice. "Or is it bad manners to talk about food right after a funeral?"

I glanced around the parking lot at the huddled groups of people engrossed in conversation. There were fewer tearful faces than I'd ever seen after a death in the community. Even Marge, flanked by Theo and Lois, looked exhausted but calm.

Alex cleared his throat, and I pulled my attention back to him.

He raised one eyebrow. "Why do I get the feeling you're not considering my etiquette question?"

I loved how he could arch his eyebrow. Why couldn't I do that? "I think once you're outside the building, anything goes. Especially since there's not a graveside service."

"In that case, how about lunch?" Alex's smile included both Carly and me.

But Carly's stare focused on something in the distance. I followed her gaze. Zac. Getting into a car with his golf teacher.

"Thanks, Alex," Carly murmured, keeping her eye on the car. "Actually, I need to run an *errand* right now." She motioned toward me. "Why don't you two go eat?"

"Another time," I said, trying my best to mimic Mama's natural grace for getting out of a sticky situation. "I'll just go with you, Car. In case you need help with your *errand*."

Alex frowned. "Why do I feel like there's a whole conversation going on that I'm not hearing?"

So I'd failed miserably in my attempt at a graceful exit. "Carly's got a lot on her mind."

Carly shook her head. "This is something I need to deal with on my own. Alex, will you drop Jenna off at home when y'all finish eating?"

"I'd be happy to."

Carly's heels click-clacked across the asphalt lot before I could frame a reply. From now on I was taking my own vehicle everywhere I went. Who'd known when my sister had offered to drive that she'd pawn me off—like a bag of old clothes for Goodwill—before the day was over? Still, short of chasing her down, I had little choice now. I was stuck going to eat with Alex.

Poor me. I could think of worse situations to be stuck in. Maybe giving in with grace would be more my thing. I smiled. "The diner?" It had been our hangout for so many years, it was hard to imagine eating anywhere else with him.

"I was going to suggest it if you didn't." He guided me toward his vehicle a few yards away.

I stopped. Even though he'd been driving a hand-me-down car from his dad when he'd left town, all these years I'd pictured him with a four-wheel-drive truck. Not the kind with oversized wheels that loomed over everything else on the highway. Alex had never been showy like that. Just a rough-and-ready truck.

Exactly like the one sitting in front of me right now.

"You don't like it?" He held the passenger door open for me.

The last thing I wanted was for him to know that he'd even crossed my mind over the years, much less that I'd imagined what kind of vehicle he drove. "It's fine."

When he slid in and buckled his seat belt, I checked mine. Alex had always been famous for going from zero to sixty in seconds. "Do you still drive like you're in NASCAR?"

"I've mellowed some over the years." He gave me a slow grin.

Great. The only thing I could imagine more dangerous to my emotional equilibrium than Alex Campbell was a mellow Alex Campbell.

When Alex and I walked into the Lake View Diner together, we automatically headed toward the booth nearest the jukebox. I slid in across from him, and for a second it was as if the hands on the big-faced clock over the counter were flying around backward, taking us back to a time when swimming practice and competitions had kept me busy. But every bit of free time I'd had, I'd spent with Alex, often in this very place. I had moved on, and so had Alex, but some memories you never outgrow.

We should have gone to McDonald's.

I scrambled for a safe topic, one not obviously stilted, yet several degrees this side of nostalgic. "How did Coach's gallbladder surgery go? In the last card I got from them, your mom mentioned he was scheduled to have it done."

"It went fine. You keep in touch with Mom and

Dad?" Alex sounded surprised.

"Why not?" I loved Alex's parents. After the Olympics, Coach must have been disappointed, especially when I decided to quit, but he hadn't made me feel bad.

"I thought—well, I wasn't sure how you felt about them after Dad practically deserted you when you didn't win." Alex picked up a menu and studied the selections with more concentration than they deserved, considering we'd had the diner's entire menu memorized fifteen years ago and it hadn't changed a whole lot since then.

I put my hand on the slightly greasy laminated card he held in front of him like a shield and pulled it down so I could see his eyes. "What exactly do you mean, deserted me? I lost, it was over, and I chose to stop. If anyone should have been disappointed, it was your dad. I failed him, not the other way around." I sounded abrupt, but I didn't want pity. Truthfully, Alex's desertion was the one that had shaken the foundation of my world. Not that I'd ever admit that to him. Hard enough to admit it to myself.

"And anyway, your parents needed to move close to your granddad—remember how sick he was? I'm sure they would have stayed here if I was still competing, but I think it may have been a relief when they were able to leave."

Alex laid the menu on the table. "I guess they didn't have much of a choice, but I never quit thinking of Lake View as home. Most of all I missed—"

"Can I get y'all something to drink?" Debbie pushed back her frosted hair with one hand and offered Alex a dazzling smile.

We agreed to try the new peach tea, and she sashayed back to the kitchen with enough twist in her step to draw almost every male eye in the place. But the man across the table kept his gaze on me. That was a good sign. Now how to nudge him back to where he was before Debbie showed up? What had he missed? The small-town atmosphere? The diner's homemade pecan pie?

"So, water girl. What's been happening in your life? Besides the obvious?"

Unfortunate fact number one: Once a conversation has been interrupted, there's no going back.

"Not much. I guess you probably know I gave up teaching a few years ago and came back home. I've been working at the health club ever since."

"I heard Bob was supposed to have sold you the place by now."

I rolled my eyes. "Of course you did. No such thing as personal business in this town, is there?" I wondered what he'd heard about why I quit teaching.

"Not last time I checked. Must make John's job easier, though. He shouldn't have any trouble finding someone willing to tell him who killed Hank and why."

Just as Alex spoke, Debbie waltzed up and plunked two tall glasses of iced peach tea down on the table. "That man sure knew how to rile people up."

I looked up at her with interest. "Hank?"

"Mm-hmm. Half of his lunch meetings ended with yelling." She lowered her voice. "Seeing as how the newspaper is right around the corner, he was a regular."

Alex nodded. "I'm sorry for your loss."

Startled, I choked on my tea. He shrugged and gave an imperceptible shake of his head, like *What was I supposed to say?*

"Who did he shout with mostly?" I asked when I'd gotten my breath back. Alex might not recognize that Debbie wanted to tell what she knew, but I sure did.

"Now that you mention it, the last person I remember him being in here with was Brendan Stiles." She leaned toward us. "You know, that new pharmacist over at Lake View Drugstore."

Apparently the fact that I'd dated said pharmacist hadn't been newsworthy enough to merit a swing on the gossip grapevine. "Yes, I know who you mean." Was it my imagination, or was Alex narrowing his eyes at me? I turned back toward Debbie. "What were they talking about?"

"I don't know." She shot a glance toward the counter, where someone's ham and cheese sitting under the heat lamp was growing staler by the minute. "Maybe Marge."

"What about Marge?" The gentle tap on my leg wasn't my imagination. Alex kicked me under the table.

"Well, I heard Hank say, 'My wife,' and then something about 'a bag.' I thought maybe Brendan was insulting Marge. But that's all I heard."

"You must hear a lot, Debbie," I said and sipped my tea.

"More than you'd believe."

"I think I'll have the turkey and dressing," Alex said.

I returned his kick.

Debbie frowned then slapped her forehead. "Of course. What was I thinking, standing here gabbing when you need to order?" She flipped her pad open and jotted down our choices, then bustled to the kitchen.

"Aren't you Chatty Cathy?" He raised an eyebrow. "Or is it Nancy Drew?"

Boy, what was it with him and Carly and the Nancy Drew thing? I ignored that part of his question and laughed. "You always said I talked too much, remember?"

"That was when I was twelve and trying to catch a fish, and you wanted to discuss the most effective swim strokes." He reached toward my hand, I think, but ended up bumping my tea glass instead.

I grabbed it to keep it from tipping over.

"You don't want to get involved in a murder investigation, Jenna."

"I don't want my nephew to go to jail for something he didn't do, Alex," I said, mocking his slightly patronizing tone.

He flicked at a speck on the plastic tablecloth. "It's my job to keep him out of jail. Don't you trust me?"

I stared at his chiseled jaw. The slight five o'clock shadow would have made most men appear unkempt and messy. Instead, it gave Alex the rugged air of a hard-working hero, too busy saving the world to shave. "I trust you." *As long as it's not my heart at risk.* From the corner of my eye, I saw Debbie enter the three-stall rest-room to the right of the kitchen.

"I'm glad to hear that." This time he connected with my hand and clasped it loosely. "I don't want you to get in over your head."

In spite of the tingle down my arm at his touch, or maybe because of it, I slipped my hand from his and pushed to my feet. "I've spent half my life in the deep end, remember? Excuse me." I wove my way through the tables to the restroom.

Debbie stood at the vanity, reapplying her lipstick. "Hey."

In the mirror, she met my eyes. "You dating Alex?"

"No."

She smacked her red lips. "I was hoping you'd say that."

I suddenly remembered hearing at the beauty shop that Debbie's husband ran off with a woman from River Falls. Sympathy warred with my desire to tell her to stay away from Alex Campbell until I decided how I felt about him.

"About Hank. If you remember more details about his conversation with Brendan, or anybody else for that matter, will you give me a holler?"

She turned the faucet on and stared at me. "I heard about your nephew. That's too bad." She squirted soap on her hands and rubbed them together under the stream. "You sure you're not dating Alex?"

"I think I'd know."

"In that case, I'll call you if I think of anything."

"Thanks." I scribbled my cell number on the back of a blank ticket for her and hurried back to my seat.

In a few minutes, Debbie brought our order. She never referred to our bathroom conversation but turned the full force of her charm on Alex. As far as I could tell, he was unaffected. I was surprised by how happy that made me.

As we were driving home, Alex glanced over at me. "You're not going to let this drop, are you?"

"Whatever do you mean?" I borrowed Carly's thickest Southern accent, the words dripping innocence.

"If I remember one thing about you, it's that once you get a bone between your teeth, you never let go."

"Are you calling me a dog?" When had I stopped engaging my brain before my mouth?

"Hardly." That one word spoke volumes.

I blushed and stared out the window.

"Promise me something," Alex said.

"What's that?" I murmured, not daring to tear my gaze away from the houses we were passing.

"At least keep me in the loop on your questions and the answers you get. As Zac's lawyer, I'd like to know anything that might affect his case."

"Oh, so this is purely professional?" The words popped out of their own accord, I promise.

"No. Not purely." He flipped on the blinker and glanced at me. "As your friend, I want to know if you're doing anything that might endanger you, too."

I nodded. Friends to the end. "Don't worry, Alex. I'm not planning on getting myself killed."

"Yeah, but here's the kicker." Alex smoothly navigated the truck into my driveway. "I'm pretty sure Hank wasn't, either."

"Point taken. I'll be discreet." I unfastened my seat belt. "Thanks for lunch."

"Let's do it again sometime."

"Sounds fun." Suddenly it felt as if I were waiting for a good-bye kiss. The thought propelled me out of the truck, and I practically ran up the sidewalk, almost tripping over the golden dog who had taken up a permanent position on my porch. Once there was a safe distance between Alex and me, I turned to wave. He was looking at me with an inscrutable expression. Probably thinking I was still crazy after all these years.

I confess I closed my eyes when I let go of the ball. But when I opened them, there wasn't a white pin standing. Again. As the electronic scoreboard excitedly flashed a big *X*, I turned to face Brendan Stiles. My date for the evening stared at the scorekeeper's monitor, his lips pinched together like someone had laced his cola with pure lemon juice.

"*Whoo-hoo!* Another strike! Sweetie, don't you want to ditch your date and join our team?" Francee Moore called to me from the next lane. "We sure could use you tonight, what with Millie Jo out sick!" She cocked an eyebrow at Brendan. "We'll let him watch!"

"You know the rules, Francee." Joyce Simms from the Shear Joy team balanced her monogrammed bowling ball on her hip and glared at Francee. "Only employees are allowed on the team."

Francee rolled her eyes at the woman in purple and yellow polyester and muttered to me, "Shear Joy should lose for sheer bad taste." She slapped one hand against the delicately intertwining *C-N-C* embroidered on her light blue and navy blouse, roughly in the direction of her heart, and ran the fingers of her other hand through her short spiked red hair. "Jenna, I promise to pay you six bucks an hour to wash hair one day a year. You choose the day. How about it?"

I could feel Brendan's gaze boring into my back. My cheeks burned. "Thanks, Francee. Looks like Cut 'n' Curl is doing fine without me, though. We're just here for fun."

And some fun it had been so far. Brendan and I were finally getting around to our date that had been postponed because of Hank's untimely demise. I'd suggested bowling, thinking a little physical activity would be better than sitting across a table, making awkward conversation. My mistake. Even tepid dinner conversation would have been an improvement over the competitive tension that had been in the air ever since we walked into the musty-smelling building. The only thing stronger than Brendan's determination to win was the magnetic pull of the gutter on his ball. He couldn't roll it straight to save his life.

"Fine. Have it your way." Francee laughed. "Joyce Sims is liable to throw that bowling ball at me if we win anyway. Sports can be dangerous."

"They sure can," a small blond beside her piped up. "One of my perms today said the police found a golf club they think someone used to kill Hank Templeton."

"Really?" I glanced at Brendan, who had abandoned his pout and was listening intently. "Whose club was it?"

"They don't know. But I reckon they're going to try to find out."

As she finished speaking, a Shear Joy team member made a strike, and pandemonium broke out.

"So a golf club was the murder weapon," I said to Brendan, then suddenly remembered what Debbie at the diner had said about Hank's heated conversation with the local pharmacist. "Did Hank play golf?" I was pretty sure he had, considering his and Marge's house backed up to the golf course, but I wanted to hear from Brendan how well he knew Hank, without asking outright.

"How should I know? I barely knew the man."

"Didn't you say you were on a zoning committee with him?"

He rolled his eyes at me. "Well, yeah. And I'm sure I saw him from a distance when I went into the news office to take out an ad for a cashier, too, but that hardly constitutes knowing him."

Neither of us mentioned the fact that Brendan

played golf. It didn't seem possible that I might be on a date with a murderer, but it was time I faced facts. Someone in our town had probably killed Hank. "You never had lunch with him or anything?" I asked, fully aware that if Alex were here, he'd be kicking me under the figurative table.

Brendan looked at me as if I'd sprouted green antennae and grown an extra head. "Me have lunch with Hank? Why would I?"

I didn't spend three years teaching school without learning to recognize an evasive answer. I also knew that sometimes you're better off to let things drop for the time being. "It's your turn to bowl."

Brendan threw two quick gutter balls then collapsed back in his seat. I picked up my ball from the rack, but his next question stopped me short.

"Maybe you should be thinking a little closer to home. Didn't you say your nephew was taking golf lessons?"

"So?"

Brendan tapped the table with the stubby pencil. "It's perfectly understandable."

I huffed. "What's understandable?"

"You're in denial."

"Denial? About Zac?" I tried to suck air into my lungs, but it felt as though they were trapped on a one-dimensional planet and refused to expand. "Zac didn't do it," I said through gritted teeth.

"Okay, whatever you say."

We'd abandoned all pretext of bowling, but I still clutched the neon green ball. I ran my hand over the slick, cool surface and fought the urge to lift it to my hot cheeks. Or better yet, slam it into Brendan's smug face. The muscles in my jaw ached. My daily Bible study was from James, and I was trying desperately to control my tongue, but biting it until it bled might be a little extreme. "I think it's time for us to call it a night." I put the ball back on the rack beside us.

Brendan pushed to his feet, the look on his face reeking of false concern. "Jenna, honey, I didn't mean to hurt your feelings, but it's true the family is often the last to know."

"I guess I'm the last to know a lot of things." I ground out the words as I changed shoes. When I'd finished, I stood and leaned toward Brendan, speaking softly for his ears only. "Like the fact that I'd rather spend every Friday night for the rest of my life at home, painting my cat's toenails, than go out with you again."

I didn't mind the walk home. The night air had never felt so cool and fresh. Some places were stale with bad company.

Lake View Monitor

HELP WANTED

Part-time position available.
Qualified applicant must have
common sense and grammar skills.
Send résumé to P.O. Box 34213,
Lake View, Arkansas 72001.
Salary commensurate with ex-
perience.

*O*omph!" Carly grunted. "That ball has it in for me." Her racket clattered to the hardwood floor. She laughed and sank down beside it. "Forget it, Jen. Racquetball isn't my game."

"You don't know that! You haven't even given it a chance." I leaned against the wall and crossed my arms, giving my sister a measured glance. "Besides, it beats staying home and moping."

Carly rubbed an angry-looking red spot on her leg. "At least staying home wasn't giving me bruises. Besides, have you ever tried to mope around ten-year-old twins? Let's call Mama and ask her how much moping she's getting done tonight."

"Nice try. Come on. Give it a few more minutes. If you still don't like it, we'll change and head to the sauna."

Carly got to her feet and waved her racket around over her head with a grin. "Boomerang ball? Crazy sister? Sauna at the end? Bring it on." She resumed the stance I'd shown her—knees slightly bent.

For the next ten minutes, she gave it her all. But when she collapsed to the floor again, gasping for air between her giggles, even I had to admit defeat.

Celebrating the end of the game, Carly did a victory dance into the locker room then collapsed onto the wooden bench across from the silver metal lockers. "Why couldn't we have played something a little less strenuous?"

"Like what? Golf?" Since finding out about the discovery of the murderous club last Friday night, Carly and I had made a list of every golfer we knew. After Carly's meeting with Elliott on the day of Hank's funeral, we weren't sure where to put him on the list. On one hand, Carly said he was charming and attractive, but on the other, there was no rule saying a killer couldn't be good-looking, was there?

But Carly's mother-tiger claws had come out when she heard what Brendan said about Zac, so the pharmacist's name was at the top of the list, circled in red. Zac, Alex, and I were at the bottom. The in-between included the golf pro, Byron, Amelia, and a good portion of Lake View's population.

"Even a deadly sport like golf is better than racquetball," Carly huffed.

I couldn't have asked for a better opening. "I'm glad you think so, because I have a plan."

She rolled her eyes. "Mercy, Jenna, how do you do it? You have more plans than Blue Cross."

"So you don't want to hear it?"

"You know I'll bite. What did you have in mind?"

"We're going to play golf this Saturday at the country club."

"We? You and me?"

I blushed. This part of my plan could be misconstrued as my having an ulterior motive. "You, me, and Alex." I pulled my swimsuit from my locker and clicked the metal door shut. "Of course, we'll need a fourth. So I've called the club and reserved their resident golf pro to play with us. That would be Elliott."

"Nancy Drew's on the case again. I can see the wheels turning. You want to get to the bottom of Elliott's fight with Hank and find out if he's missing a golf club."

"That's the plan in a nutshell."

"Works for me." Carly picked up her towel. "Somehow I can't see him as a killer, but I think we do need to get to know him a little better."

"Exactly." I was relieved that she wasn't putting up a fight. But a little surprised.

"Have you mentioned this to Alex?"

"No, but he'll go along with it." I fiddled with my swimsuit strap.

"Oh my. One post-funeral lunch date and you're pretty confident of your charms, aren't you?" She gave me a wide grin.

"Not really, but he did say to keep him up-to-date on my investigation."

Carly popped me with her towel. "Get outta here. He was okay with you playing Jenna Stafford, Girl Detective?"

"Once he realized he couldn't stop me, I guess he figured better to be in the loop than out of it."

"Smart man. When is tee time?"

"Elliott's supposed to meet us there at 7:00 a.m."

"Just thinking about getting out on the greens that early makes me look forward to a lazy sauna session right now," Carly drawled.

After we stretched out on benches in the empty sauna room, Carly covered her eyes with her extra towel. I did the same and allowed the quiet humidity to penetrate the sore places of my soul.

"I needed this."

I raised a corner of my towel and saw Carly peering at me across the dimly lit room. "Thanks for dragging me out of the house," she murmured and let her towel back down over her eyes.

"I'm glad you came."

For several minutes, the only sound in the room was our breathing.

Then Carly broke the silence. "You know, I haven't been attracted to any man since Travis left." Long pause. "Until now."

Shock kept me quiet.

"But there's something different about Elliott. And he acted like he felt the same about me."

Sweat trickled between my shoulder blades, and I

rubbed my back against the nubby towel.

"Wow." I didn't know what else to say.

"I know. It's weird." I heard her shift on the boards. "And why would someone like him be interested in me? He probably makes every woman feel that way."

"Carly, don't be ridiculous. Of course he'd be interested in you. Any man in his right mind would be."

"Let's just drop it, okay?" Even in the dark I could tell Carly was embarrassed by her confession.

"Okay."

Silence reigned.

When I'd enjoyed all the soul soothing I could stand, I pushed to a sitting position. "Did you see the ad in the paper?"

"Uh-uh," Carly answered without opening her mouth or moving her towel.

From the sound of her voice, I could tell she was in no hurry to join me in the land of the sitting, but I can only take so much inactivity. "You didn't? For the job at the paper?"

"Oh. Yeah, I saw that. So?" Carly tucked the towel tighter around her eyes.

"So?" I lifted her towel, and one brown eye glared at me. "So I thought one of us should apply."

Carly sat up. She wiped the sweat from her face and neck and looked at me like I was out of my mind. "Why?"

I rolled my eyes. "So we could be at the newspaper office. . .undercover."

Carly shook her head. "From Nancy Drew to

Charlie's Angel in one fell swoop. I'm not doing it."

"Fine. I will."

"You're going to send a résumé?"

"No, actually, I thought I'd stop by tomorrow and talk to Marge." As the last few words came out of my mouth, the sauna room door opened.

Amelia Stanton breezed into the dimly lit room, her neon-orange bikini reminding me of fog lights. Carly sat up and shot me a look. Had Amelia heard us?

We didn't have to wonder long.

"Hi, dears." Amelia arranged an extra-thick towel on the bench and sank down, covering her eyes with another one. "I wish *I* could visit Marge. But unfortunately, she doesn't want to see me."

I gave a mental groan. What could we say to that? "Really? I'm sorry to hear that." I tried a trick I'd learned from John and made the end of the sentence sound like a question, hoping to trigger an explanation.

"Yes," Amelia said, her voice more languid. "She blames me for Hank's death, or at least Byron, and me by extension."

"Why?" Enough tricks. My direct question hung in the damp hot air.

"Nancy Drew," Carly mouthed at me and narrowed her eyes.

"Who knows?" Amelia rearranged her towel. "When we were younger, Marge and I were as close as you two. But then we drifted apart. We might have patched it up, but after we married. . ." She folded her hands across her taut stomach. "Well, I never blamed her. A woman has to stand by her husband. Even if he's wrong."

I raised an eyebrow at Carly. "Hank came between you?"

"Oh my. That's an understatement."

I wondered if the reclining position combined with my clinical-questioning technique reminded Amelia of talking with her psychiatrist, because the words kept pouring out.

"He hated Byron." Even though we were the only ones in the room, she lowered her voice to a conspiratorial whisper. "Almost from the day we married."

"So I guess it's a relief to you in a way that he's gone?"

Carly put her hand to her mouth and bit back a choking cough. I ignored her.

Amelia was quiet for a few seconds, and I was afraid she was going to tell me to mind my own business, but when she spoke, her voice was soft. "It was like winning the lottery. Or at least it would be, if Marge would allow me back into her life."

Carly made a cutting motion across her neck, but I averted my gaze from her and took the big plunge. "Do you have any idea who might have killed him?"

"My stars, honey. How would I know? Hank had more enemies than a Saks Fifth Avenue has dressing rooms."

Carly stood and motioned frantically to me that we needed to go.

I ignored her. "Byron must have hated Hank, as well."

Amelia pulled the towel back from her eyes, and

Carly froze in mid-motion. "Hank put Byron through hell. But Byron didn't kill him." Every ounce of ditzy blond was gone as Amelia leveled a steely gaze on me. "And believe me, Jenna Stafford, if you try to pin it on him, you'll be sorry."

Carly latched onto my arm. "Amelia, it's been nice talking to you. I hope you and Marge work things out. Mama's got the twins, and we have to go." She tossed an artificial laugh over her shoulder as she shoved me out of the room. "Can't be late for our curfew."

As soon as we were back in the locker room, I swung around to glare at Carly. "Why did you do that? She was spilling her guts."

"Oh yeah. I could see that." Carly met my glare and added a touch of sarcasm to her own. "In between threatening to spill *your* guts if you don't butt out."

"She didn't say that." I snatched up a towel and headed for the showers.

"Jenna, maybe you need to rethink the whole 'common sense' requirement of that newspaper ad. What part of 'You'll be sorry' do you not understand?"

I spun to face her. "Car, I just want to clear Zac."

Carly's shoulders slumped. "So do I. But you scare me. You have to be more careful."

"If you would help me, then you could keep me out of trouble."

Carly laughed. "Nice try, sis. It would take an army to keep you out of trouble once you set your head to playing detective."

"But you'll help me?"

"Was there ever any doubt?" Carly brushed past me and headed for the showers.

Déjà vu. Standing outside Marge's door with food. Again. I nervously clutched the pot of Carly's cheesy Mexican broccoli soup. Too bad Mama wasn't with me to make sure I said the right thing. Maybe the food would speak louder than words. Carly and I figured the funeral fare had been either eaten or ruined by now. With only herself to feed, Marge could heat this up one bowlful at a time.

Footsteps sounded on the hardwood floor, and the ornate door creaked open. "Jenna, honey, come in." Her kiss on my cheek enveloped me in the sweet scent of spearmint. I returned her embrace, shocked by how fragile she felt. As if a hug would crush her.

"How are you?"

"Okay, I guess. Hasn't sunk in yet, I don't think." This was a much more subdued, less manic Marge than when we'd brought food before the funeral. Dark circles underlined her bloodshot eyes, and when she brushed her hair back from her face with a trembling hand, a stray tear splashed down her face. "Why would someone do such a thing to Hank?"

Motive wasn't a problem. I could think of five reasons right off the top of my head why someone would kill Hank, but those aren't the things you share with grieving widows. So I shrugged. "It's a strange world out there." I patted her arm awkwardly. *Carly is so much better at this than I am. I should have let her skip the funeral and come here with me instead.* How did I miss out on the sympathetic, knowing-just-what-to-say gene?

Life's not fair.

And that sad fact was even more evident when Marge and I sat down in the darkened living room. The quiet of the house covered us like a blanket. No football playing on the TV or local news blasting from the radio. No Hank calling for a glass of tea. No wonder Marge was going bananas.

"Are you sleeping well?"

She twisted a tissue in her hands. "Not really."

"Can't you get Doc Brown to give you something?" I remembered how much perkier she'd been when we'd come over with food before the funeral. I'd thought she'd acted weird then, and maybe under the influence, but now—in my humble, nonmedical opinion—a little more of whatever she'd been taking that day seemed to be in order.

She shredded the tissue into strips as if she were about to embark on a papier-mâché adventure, then peered up at me, looking much older than her sixty-something years. "I'd rather feel the pain than lose who I am."

"I understand, but—"

Her trembling hand closed on mine. "You're a sweet girl, Jenna. I appreciate you."

"Thanks, Marge." I cleared my throat. What I was

about to do bordered on taking advantage—and I had to admit that clearing Zac's name was my biggest motivator. Still, if I could find the murderer and, by doing that, give Marge peace, my conscience could stand the hammering. "I noticed you had an ad in the paper for a part-time position." I smiled gently. "I have good grammar skills and at least a little common sense."

"Why didn't I think of that?" Marge murmured, almost as if she were talking to herself. "I know you were a coach, but didn't you teach, too?"

"Yes, ma'am." Physical education and swimming, but does she really need to know that?

"You'd be perfect."

"Really?" All of my persuasive arguments, along with the crisp résumé in my purse—useless. Was there such a thing as too easy? "What does the position entail?"

"Before I tell you, you have to give me your word that you won't share this secret with anyone."

"Does that include Carly? If I can guarantee she won't repeat it?" I knew myself. I was going to tell Carly whatever it was. And I had enough guilt for taking advantage of Marge's grief. I wasn't about to start out our professional relationship by lying to her.

Marge seemed to think it over, then sighed. "No one should be expected to keep a secret from her sister. Especially not when they're close. You can tell Carly. But no one else. Agreed?" In the dim light, the firm set of her jaw reminded me of Hank. Maybe she wasn't as fragile as she seemed.

I agreed, and for the next ten minutes, Marge allowed

me into the magical, mysterious world of the local advice columnist, Dear Prudence, also known as Dear Pru. Dear Pru was required to sign a legally binding confidentiality contract promising to keep his or her identity secret or face legal consequences. Hank had to let the last Dear Pru go due to irresponsible answers. He'd been handling the letters himself for the last few weeks.

Marge was anxious to fill the position, and before I left her house, I had a key to the newspaper office and a part-time job moonlighting at the paper. Literally. Eventually I would do most of my work from home, but in the beginning I'd be using the letters already received and sorted in a file at the office. While there, I could look through the past questions and answers to familiarize myself with the job. I agreed to work during that rare time no one was at the office—Tuesday nights after five. Marge officially hired me for a night-shift typist position I could use as a cover in the unlikely event someone ran into me then.

My mind reeled with the possibilities by the time I got to my car. In order to go undercover to investigate the newspaper office, I'd just taken an undercover job working for the newspaper. Did that make me a double agent? Or a crazy woman with more curiosity than brains?

Lake View Monitor

Dear Prudence,

My fiancé's job requires him to be outside on his feet all day. We hardly ever go out or do the fun things we used to do. Even though he says he still loves me, he wants to rent a movie and order takeout every night. He claims this is an investment in our future—that he's working extra hard to build his reputation and his schedule will smooth out later. But my life is boring and empty. What should I do?

~Lonely in Lake View

Dear Lonely,

Don't waste time waiting for a man to make you happy. Get a life. Take charge of your own destiny and lose the loser.

~Prudence

When Carly and I arrived at the country club early Saturday morning, Alex and Elliott were standing beside two golf carts at the edge of the course, chatting like old friends. Alex waved and motioned us over, then went back to talking. Elliott, strikingly handsome, in a broad-shouldered Pierce Brosnan way, seemed genuinely interested in Alex's conversation. I never would have guessed he was getting paid for his time if I wasn't the one paying him.

"They look as though they stepped off the pages of *Golf Digest*," I muttered to Carly as we walked through the breezeway toward the men. "And here I am, straight from the clearance section in Uniforms 'R' Us."

"Oh, sweetie, you'd look good in anything." Carly looked down at herself. "I don't know why I wore this. I'm a walking flag. One of those extra-large ones."

"You silly goose, you could double for a finalist in the Miss Fourth of July pageant." For some unknown reason, Carly had decided to go patriotic today. Red, white, and blue from her stars-and-stripes sun visor down to her little flag-adorned red toenails peeking out of her walking sandals. I teased her, but I had to admit the ensemble looked good on her.

My closet hadn't yielded anything nearly as coordinated or snazzy. Last time Francee cut my hair, she mentioned that royal blue makes my eyes "pop," so I threw on a royal blue polo shirt with my favorite pair of khakis. Unfortunately, her fashion advice backfired when I walked into the club this morning and realized I was dressed exactly like the greens maintenance crew, sans the monogram above the shirt pocket.

"Are we supposed to get some clubs at the desk?"

"No—I reserved them, but Alex said he'd pick them up."

Carly nudged me. "So is this your second date?"

I snorted. "It better not be, considering I'm the one who asked him to come, and I'm paying the greens fee and club rental. Besides, the first one wasn't a date, either. He asked both of us, but you—"

"Methinks thou dost protest too much," Carly interrupted, in that smarmy way of big sisters everywhere. She looped her arm in mine and whispered in my ear, "You're babbling."

I had no chance to deny it, because we'd reached the men. I hadn't allowed myself to think of the personal implications when I'd called Alex and asked him to play golf with us. But faced with being close to him, in a situation of my own engineering, my knees trembled. His heart-stopping smile didn't help.

He introduced me to Elliott, and I shook the man's hand while trying to take his measure as a person. Not an easy thing with a quick handshake. Did he look like a killer? No. But I'd come to the sad conclusion that Hank's murderer may very well not be sporting an ear-to-lip scar and an evil grin.

When Elliott shook Carly's hand, he didn't let go immediately. "It's great to see you again. Zac talks about you so much, I feel like I already know you."

Like Carly was going to be taken in by that line. Zac loved his mom, but at sixteen, he wasn't going to be talking about her to his golf instructor. And we both knew it.

Carly snatched her hand away, and her face turned as red as a flag stripe. She stammered, "Thanks. Good to see you again, too."

Unlike me, my sister is unrattleable when it comes to the opposite sex. Going through trial by fire with Travis seemed to sear her what-will-a-man-think? nerve. Or so I'd always thought—until today. But she was obviously more than a little shaken by her attraction to the smooth golf pro.

My hackles rose. Did this man, who very well may have killed Hank and charmed my nephew into allowing himself to be blamed for it, now conspire to seduce my sister so that she wouldn't recognize him for what he was? "Elliott, I'm so glad you were available to work today," I said, stepping neatly between my sister and the murder-minded Don Juan.

"Thanks. Wouldn't have missed it." Instead of being angry at my rudeness, Elliott sounded like he meant it.

Alex put his hand on my arm. "Shall we get started?"

We played the first hole quickly. It was a long par three, but that didn't stop Elliott from getting a birdie. "Show off," I muttered under my breath while Carly cheered. Hadn't she ever heard that in golf you were supposed to clap quietly and say, "Ahh," when someone did well?

Thrilled with her beginner's-luck bogey, Carly allowed Elliott to guide her to the front golf cart, where he solicitously helped her get settled into the passenger seat then went around and hopped in behind the wheel. As Alex and I were loading into our cart, he shot me a sideways glance. "What's the deal? I've never seen you be so rude."

"A golf club killed Hank Templeton," I hissed. "Zac told us Elliott had a huge fight with Hank before the murder. Do you want to see Carly taken in by a killer?"

"No," Alex whispered as he guided us along the cart path, "but I find it hard to believe he's the killer."

"And you're basing that on what? A five-minute conversation with him this morning?"

"Actually, he eats breakfast with us at the diner."

"And the fact that he tolerates Alice's cooking exonerates him?"

He ran a hand through his short blond hair and sighed. "Jenna, if you're going to play detective—not that I'm advocating that—but if you are, you're going to have to learn to keep your cool." We slowly puttered toward the second hole, where Elliott and Carly were already picking out their clubs. "If he is the murderer, you've tipped him off to your suspicion immediately. Is that what you want?"

At the clear sound of worry in his voice, my anger fizzled out like a bottle-rocket dud, and my face burned. "Obviously not. I just can't stand to think of someone taking advantage of Carly after it's taken her so long to rebuild her life."

"Come to think of it, he asked me about her before Hank's murder, so maybe he really likes her." He pulled our cart up beside Carly and Elliott's, effectively ending the discussion.

After playing three holes of the nine-hole course, Carly grabbed a paper cone from the cooler and filled it with water. "Break time," she announced and plopped down into one of the side-by-side golf carts. I grabbed my own water and took the open spot beside her before Elliott could. I'd tolerated his and Carly's banter, but I still didn't trust him completely. Alex sent me an I-know-what-you're-up-to look as he and Elliott sat in the cart beside us.

"Did y'all hear that the police think Hank was killed with a golf club?" I asked the air in general.

Carly squirmed a little beside me. She'd been gung ho when I'd planned this, but clearly her interest in Elliott was coloring her willingness to play detective.

"I heard that." Alex said Carly's rehearsed line, even though he hadn't been in on our planning. I could have kissed him. I pulled myself from fantasyland and jumped back into the script.

"Wonder whose club it was?" I watched Elliott's face closely, not expecting an answer but wanting to see his reaction.

He stood abruptly, crushed his empty water cone in his fist, and tossed it in the trash barrel. I got out of his cart and climbed into mine by Alex. When we reached the next hole, Elliott stomped up to the tee box, his expression dark. "This is actually none of your business, and I'm only telling you because I know you're worried about Zac, but the police came here this week asking questions." He glanced at Carly. "They think the murder weapon was one of our rentals."

I waved my own driver. "Like this?"

"Yes."

"So it should be easy enough to check the records and see who didn't turn their club back in, shouldn't it?" Alex asked. His tone was casual, but he stepped slightly between Elliott and me. My hero.

"Not necessarily. Think about it. If you were a clerk making six dollars an hour, would you worry about making sure missing clubs are accounted for?" He waved a hand toward the wide expanse of rolling hills. "We find them out on the greens all the time." Either he deserved an Emmy or he was an innocent man. Right now, in my book, it was a toss-up.

"So it's the perfect murder weapon," I said.

"Ew," Carly interjected. "No such thing." She placed her ball in the tee box, stepped back, and took a practice swing.

"No, Jenna's right," Alex mused. "Untraceable, not belonging to any one person. It's not like they can investigate the country club as a murder suspect." He walked over to slide an iron from his bag.

No, but they could take the country club's golf pro in for questioning. "Did the police talk to you personally?"

Elliott looked at me, then at Carly, who had stopped mid-swing. "Yes, they did. I had an argument with Hank a few weeks before his murder."

"What about?" I fiddled with my wristband and pretended the question was normal.

Elliott's tanned face reddened. "I felt that his newspaper mishandled a personal matter."

"Did he agree?"

"Actually, he did promise to take care of the person

responsible." Elliott clutched his iron with white knuckles. "Are we here today for you to question me? Or is there any chance you want to play golf?" He sounded more resigned than angry, and I felt bad. He'd been more forthcoming than I would have been if faced with such interrogation.

Carly took her position at the tee box, refusing to look at me. "Y'all, if they'd put a windmill down there by the cup, I just know I could get a hole-in-one."

Elliott's face relaxed, and Alex grinned. Carly had effectively defused the situation, and I had no doubt my who?-li'l-ole-me? sister had done it on purpose.

"Or maybe a little doghouse with a door to hit the ball through?" I joined in.

"Just use your imagination," Elliott coached.

Carly promptly hit her ball out of bounds.

"I don't think he meant for you to close your eyes, Car," I teased.

Elliott eyed Alex and me. "I'd say that calls for a mulligan, wouldn't y'all?"

"Sure," Alex answered quickly.

"What's a mulligan?" I asked, convinced that Alex didn't know what it was, either, but in the tradition of men everywhere refused to admit his ignorance.

"Yeah, because if it's a sandwich, especially a break-fast one, that sounds good." Carly glared in the direction of her missing ball.

Elliott laughed, and so did Alex, so maybe he did know what it was.

"A mulligan is a do-over. When you're playing with

friends, you can get a chance to do it over if everyone agrees." Elliott grinned at Carly.

"A sandwich would be better. But she can definitely do it over." I smiled. Elliott was being a remarkably good sport. The least I could do was try to be one, too. I could always move him up on the suspect list later if I needed to.

Carly's inexperience balanced Elliott's professional status; plus, after his initial burst of irritation, he was holding back a little, so by the eighth hole, we were about even.

"What's the par on this one?" I asked, adjusting my royal blue cap and scoping out the shot.

"Three." Alex smiled.

"Sounds like the perfect place for me to make a birdie."

"You dream big, don't you?"

"Nothing wrong with that, is there?" I swung with all my might, and the ball flew for a good distance then dropped to the ground, just short of the green.

"Oh no!" Carly stamped her foot.

"Who's your partner, me or her?" Elliott asked her, laughing. Then he turned to me. "Don't worry about it—you're still doing great."

"Easy for you to say." I grinned, hoping he would accept it as an apology for earlier. "But thanks."

"No problem."

A few minutes later, on the way to the next hole, Alex slowed to a stop and looked over at me. Carly and Elliott's cart disappeared over the hill, and no one else was in sight.

I'd been thinking about who killed Hank, but Alex's intense gaze sent the mystery fleeing from my mind. "What?"

"You still pouting about missing that birdie?"

"Nah. It wasn't even close." I shivered. Not nearly as close as his face to mine.

"People don't always get it right on the first try, water girl." Alex leaned a little closer, and I was pretty sure we weren't talking about golf anymore. "Sometimes things worth having are worth a second shot, don't you agree?" he whispered.

My heart pounded in my throat, and I nodded.

He sat back in his seat. "Good." He pushed the pedal and buzzed along merrily to the last hole, keeping his attention on the path.

Forget murder. My heart may not survive another shot with Alex Campbell.

Lake View Monitor

MURDER INVESTIGATION

Local police are investigating the recent murder of Hank
Templeton, but no arrests have
been made. "We are following
every lead," says Police Chief
John Conner. He declined to
comment on the cause of death,
although sources report that a
murder weapon was found. "Mr.
Templeton's body was sent to
the Arkansas State Crime Lab
at Little Rock for an autopsy,"
the chief added.

You know, the first few weeks Alex was back in town, I didn't see him at all, but now, everywhere I go, there he is." The alley seemed to grow darker and more menacing as I fumbled with the key to the back door of the newspaper office.

Carly followed my gaze to the right. "Church on Sunday and the diner last night. That's not really everywhere you go. You didn't see him at work today. . . ."

Her voice, already distracted, drifted off.

I froze with the key in the lock. "Is that something moving?"

Carly clutched my arm, and we peered into the narrow alley alongside the red-brick building. A long line of tall evergreen shrubs shielded the dark thoroughfare from the park. I looked behind us at the guard light shining down on my car in the paved lot adjoining Main Street Park, mentally measuring the distance. *Maybe we should make a break for it.*

A calico cat darted out of the alley, followed closely by a gray tabby. They disappeared into the park. I let out my breath, and Carly released my arm with a nervous giggle.

"Whew. We have to get a grip," Carly whispered as I turned the key in the lock and pushed open the door.

"Yeah, I'd planned on not turning on many lights, but I think we need a new plan." I flipped on the light switches and lit up the back half of the building. From the road, a passerby wouldn't be able to see these lights, but it was enough illumination to shove away the last of the creepy feeling we'd had.

Five minutes later, we found the Dear Pru file exactly where Marge told me it would be, in Hank's office. We sat down, one on each side of the desk, and I spread the letters out in front of us.

I picked up one out of last month's archives and began to read aloud. " 'Dear Pru, I get no respect around here. What do you think I should do?' Signed, 'Trampled.' "

"Is there an answer?" Carly asked.

I nodded. " 'Dear Trampled, respect can't be asked for; it has to be demanded. You're only trampled if you let yourself be. So stand up and be counted.' "

"Hmm. Blunt, but I guess that makes sense. This is going to be kind of hard, isn't it?" Carly held up a current letter. " 'Dear Prudence, I'm fourteen and my parents won't give me any privacy. I'm a good kid, but they think because I'm a teenager I'm automatically bad. What should I do?' Signed, 'Need Some Space.' "

"Oh, that's a good one. Put it over to the side for me to answer later." I was hoping to start on some fairly easy ones. And garner some wisdom from the previous Dear Prudences.

Carly jerked. "What's that noise?" The popping sound followed by creaking noises echoed in the quiet, empty building.

"I think it's the heater coming on. Let's don't get all jumpy again." I was nervous, too, but I wouldn't mention that to Carly. "We have a right to be here, remember?" And if anyone saw us here, well, I was an employee.

"*You* have a right to be here, not me." Technically, Carly was right, but even though I was acting bravely, I was really glad she was here with me.

"Don't be silly. You're my assistant."

"Without pay, right?"

"Yes, but with a lot of honor. So, honored assistant, how many unopened letters are there?"

She shuffled through them. "About ten."

"Marge said there would be between five and fifteen every week. They're all local, so at least it's not like a deluge of letters." I'd envisioned huge mailbags before Marge had told me that little tidbit. Apparently the citizens of Lake View didn't need advice all that much. Or if they did, they didn't realize it.

"That doesn't give you much to choose from if you answer three each week." She ripped another one open. " 'Dear Prudence, my husband thinks if we exchange all our lightbulbs for long-lasting ones, we'll save loads of money. I think it's wasteful to throw away a bulb that hasn't burned out yet. What do you think?' Signed, 'In the Dark.' "

I rolled my eyes. "Trash," we said together, and Carly tossed it in the round metal can by the desk.

For the next several minutes, we pored over the letters and replies, reading bits aloud. After I'd gathered the current ones to take home and try to answer and a few of the archives for reference, I lowered my voice. "We'd better start looking if we're going to find any clues to Hank's murder."

I flipped on the computer.

"What are you doing?" Carly walked over to stand behind me.

"I just want to check his history. I'm sure the police already did, but maybe we'll see something they missed."

"Won't you need a password?"

I pointed at the screen. "Thankfully, Hank saved it." I logged on and pulled up his history for the last twenty days. There were the usual Web sites—weather, sports, news. No pornography or online gambling sites had been visited within the last twenty days.

"Look at this flyer I found stuck in the Dear Pru archives." Carly held up a bright yellow brochure. "'Makeover for Couples! Two-for-One Special at the Luxury Spa in Memphis, Thursday, September 5 through Sunday, September 8. Surprise your Special Someone with a spa weekend featuring Botox and collagen injections in the privacy of your Luxury suite with your own personal attendant. Tanning beds, permanent makeup, and elimination of spider veins and unsightly age spots included. No need to grow old together gracefully when you can stay young for each other forever.'"

I looked up from the computer. "Weird. Marge said Hank was handling Dear Pru when he died. I guess he stuck that in there. Maybe he was going to surprise Marge."

She shuddered. "Eww. Can you see Hank and Marge getting makeovers?"

Before I could answer, my cursor moved to the more recent sites in the computer's history and I gasped. "Look at this. Oh my goodness. Why would he have all these? There are at least a hundred sites about prescription drugs."

"Must be for a story."

"I'm sure. But about what?"

"Drugs?" Carly chuckled. "Just a guess, Nancy Drew."

The rest of the history showed nothing important,

so I shut down the computer.

"I'll look through the file cabinet and you check his desk."

I slid open the first metal drawer and stared at the file tabs. Most of them didn't seem pertinent. Then my gaze fell on a tab marked CURRENT EDITORIALS. I plucked it from the drawer.

"Listen to this. This was the editorial that was supposed to go out the week after Hank died. It's not completely done, but listen." I waved the paper in Carly's face. " 'Our esteemed mayor is up to his eyebrows in more than the citizens of Lake View can ever imagine.' What do you think Hank meant by that?"

"No idea. Oh, you should read this letter. 'I'm sixteen and my parents are so out of touch. I feel like I can't talk to them about anything.' Isn't that just so sad?" Carly hadn't moved from her chair, still enthralled with the Dear Pru letters.

"Carly, stop reading those letters and help me look."

She reluctantly left the letters, and we opened every drawer of Hank's massive, battle-scarred oak desk. If there were any clues there, we weren't smart enough to find them.

"Let's take a break and have a cup of coffee. Newspaper offices are known for having coffee, right?" In the break room, Carly put some fresh coffee in the Brewmaster and I poked around in the cabinets.

"Ever wonder what newspaper employees keep in their refrigerator?" Carly opened the door and peered inside. "Ketchup, mustard, and French vanilla creamer. That's it."

"Glad you cleared up that little mystery for me." I took two cups off the shelf and filled them with hot coffee. "Check out the freezer—maybe there's some Häagen-Dazs or Ben & Jerry's."

"Nope. Just some ice and a brown paper bag." Carly shut the freezer door and sipped her coffee.

"What's in the bag?"

"Are you serious?" Carly asked.

"Sure. Maybe it's cold cash."

Carly opened the door, retrieved the bag, and shook the frost off it. "Looks like medicine of some kind." She pulled out several prescription bottles and set them on the table. "Oxycontin. Isn't that a prescription painkiller?"

I shook one. Empty. I shook another one. Empty, too. Every bottle was empty. "The label says ANNE MANSFIELD. Who's that?"

"No idea. This one's for Josephine Winston," Carly said, showing me the one she held. "Never heard of her, either. You?"

"Nope."

We sorted them out by names and ended up with three for Josephine, four for Anne. "Who would be sick enough to gather up different women's empty pill bottles?"

"Maybe there was some kind of plastic drive and we just didn't hear about it? A recycle-your-old-pill-bottles thing? And these accidentally got put in the freezer instead of with the others?"

"But they're all painkillers," I mused.

Carly nodded and ran her finger over the bottle label. "Why would anyone have these?"

"I don't know. Unless it was for a story Hank was doing. The one he did the Web research for. They're all from Lake View Pharmacy and all dated within the last few months."

"Oh well, it was more interesting than ice cream but not near as tasty." Carly shoved the bottles back into the sack and started to put them back in the freezer.

"Wait. Maybe I should take them to Marge and ask her if she knows what they're for."

"If you think these have anything to do with Hank's murder, you need to take them straight to John." Carly sounded like the bossy older sister she was.

"If they did, don't you think John would have confiscated them when the police searched this place?" I scribbled the names from the labels on the outside of my folder and stuffed the bag back into the freezer.

The heat kicked off with a loud *pop,* and Carly jumped. "C'mon, girl. Let's clean up this mess and get out of here. I've enjoyed about all of this place I can stand."

She might be a tad on the bossy side, but in this case, I completely agreed with her.

Two hours later, I pulled my old threadbare terry robe around me and sat down on the love seat with the Dear Prudence file. I sketched out some rough-draft answers to a couple of letters then pulled one out of the archive. The previous Dear Prudence had been much more forceful with her advice than I was. Was that good or bad? I scanned the letter and then read it again more carefully. Could it be? I scooped up the cordless and punched in Carly's cell number. She answered on the fourth ring. "Tell me this is important."

"Already in bed?"

"Hmm. It's ten thirty. I have to get up at six. Yes, as lazy at it seems to you, I'm in bed." She cleared her throat and laughed. "But I'm awake now. So what's up?"

"I need you to listen to this Dear Prudence letter."

"I thought I was the one addicted to them—"

I didn't let her finish. " 'Dear Prudence, my fiancé's job requires him to be outside on his feet all day. We hardly ever go out or do the fun things we used to do. Even though he says he still loves me, he just wants to rent a movie and order takeout every night. He claims this is an investment in our future—that he's working extra hard to build his reputation and his schedule will smooth out later. But my life is boring and empty. What should I do?' It's signed 'Lonely in Lake View'!"

"Fascinatin'," Carly drawled. "Sounds like she's got some serious growing up to do. And this is worth waking me up for because. . . ?"

"It has to be written by Elliott's fiancée." I'd not been surer of anything since we'd started trying to solve this mystery.

"How do you figure that?"

"Listen to the answer. 'Don't waste time waiting for a man to make you happy. Get a life. Take charge of your own destiny and lose the loser.' "

"Ouch."

"Remember what Zac said about Elliott's girlfriend leaving over something to do with the newspaper? If an anonymous columnist gave your fiancée that kind of advice and she left you, wouldn't you confront the editor?"

"Probably. But I wouldn't kill him." Carly was definitely wide-awake now and apparently remembering the chemistry between her and the handsome golf pro.

"You would if you were obsessed with the woman. And a little bit psycho."

Silence.

"Carly, I'm sorry. I know he seems nice, but we have to consider all the possibilities."

"Yeah, you may be right. Move him to the top of the list for now."

I hung up feeling lower than a snake's belly. My sister deserved whatever happiness she could find, and for all I knew, Elliott was a fine Christian man. But she was right. For now, he belonged at the top of our suspect list.

Lake View Monitor

LOST AND FOUND

Found: Male golden retriever,
Fri., Sept. 6, near Main Street
Park. If you have information
about this dog, call (870)
555-3232 and leave a message.

I could sleep through a lot of noises. Dripping faucet, worn-out refrigerator motor, Neuro snoring. But even I couldn't sleep soundly enough to ignore a dog howling outside the front door at four in the morning.

I threw back the comforter and slipped on the Tweety Bird slippers Carly had bought me as some kind of sick prank on Neuro. I don't think they bothered the cat, but Carly got a kick out of them. Neuro raised her head and blinked sleepily at me from her position at the foot of the bed. I stumbled down the hall to the front door. The cat, wide-awake now, was hot on my heels.

I stopped, hand on the knob. What if someone were torturing that poor dog so I'd unlock my door in the middle of the night? The howls were bloodcurdling. With a murderer on the loose in Lake View, a girl couldn't be too careful. I peeked out the window. The golden retriever was so pressed against my front door, he was barely visible, but I knew he was there by the endless off-key song. Persistence. I admired that in people, but it was downright annoying in a dog.

I'd put cat food out for him the last couple of days, praying he wouldn't get sick. Other than his ceaseless attempts to get into the house, he seemed happy enough. He didn't even bark at Neuro anymore, and I'm almost positive I caught them rubbing noses through the window last night.

So why howl now? I couldn't help but suspect he'd calculated his odds of catching me in that particular sleep-deprived state that will make a person do almost anything to go back to la-la land. And as bad as I hated to admit it, he'd chosen his time wisely.

I picked Neuro up and opened the front door. For a brief second, he hesitated, then bounded into the house. Neuro stiffened and snuggled closer to me. I reached out one hand to pat the dog on the head. "Will the laundry room do, Mr. Persistence?"

He chuffed in what I hoped was agreement.

"I'll have to shut the door." I resisted the urge to talk anymore. If I got too awake, I'd take him back outside where he belonged. A couple of dirty towels made a soft bed, and I filled an empty Cool Whip dish with water. He drank a little, then chased his tail around in a circle and collapsed on the towels, smiling. "Good night, Mr. Persi," I said softly and closed the door.

When it was time to get up and start the day, I was stunned to find no mess in the laundry room. And even more surprised when Neuro leaped from my arms and padded over to the golden-haired dog. I held my breath while they sniffed the air and two-stepped around each other. Mr. Persi gave a bounding leap toward Neuro, landing playfully on his haunches. The cat jumped back but then slowly initiated the dance again. I laughed aloud, and it felt good. Chaos all around and order in the strangest places.

I put Mr. Persi in the fenced-in backyard with cat food and water and loaded Neuro in her carrier for our daily trek, then paid a surprise visit to the police station before work to show John the Dear Pru letter. After he finished laughing, I tried to explain about Elliott and his girlfriend, but our very important chief of police left for a very important meeting, muttering something about "nosy women needing to learn to mind their own business."

If the police weren't going to do their job, that only left me. And Carly. Unfortunately, my sweet-tempered sis can morph into a mule at the oddest times. I cradled the cordless phone against my shoulder and sprayed window cleaner on the floor-to-ceiling mirror in the workout room. "C'mon, Carly. You know we've got to talk to him sooner or later."

We needed to ask Elliott some key questions—if we could think of any—to try to mark him off our so-called list of suspects. The attraction between him and Carly could be a wonderful breakthrough for her. Or it could be a disaster. I, for one, did not intend to let my sister lose her heart to a murderer.

"Doesn't it seem a tad bit strange to just walk in and accuse a man of murder?"

"We're not going to accuse anyone. You know better than that." I wiped the mirror with circular motions that reminded me too much of how this conversation was going.

"I know *I'm* not. You, I'm not so sure about."

"I promise, Car. I'm not going to be confrontational. It'll be a friendly little information-gathering visit."

"Fine! I'll go, but if you embarrass me, you'll pay. And I mean it, Jenna Stafford."

I grinned. When we were growing up, if I ever tattled on her or hid behind the couch and made kissy noises at her and her date, I could always be sure that she'd get me back. Greased shower nozzle, short-sheeted bed, salted toilet seat—she was the master of payback. I wasn't willing to take a chance on the assumption that she'd outgrown such stunts. I'd handle Elliott with kid gloves.

"I'll behave. Pick you up at lunch?"

"I'll be ready."

An hour later, she climbed into my car and I turned toward the country club. I glanced over at her. "How should we handle this? Should we act casual? Or let him know what we're there for?"

"I called and told him we wanted to come by and talk about Hank's murder." She placed her hands primly in her lap and looked out the window.

My mouth dropped open. "You did?"

She shrugged one shoulder. "I figured he deserved to know up front what we were doing."

That would undoubtedly be more welcome than my surprise attack. "Good." I pulled up under the club breezeway.

Carly sighed. "I dread Zac's reaction when he finds out I told Elliott what he said."

"You could ask Elliott not to tell him."

"I could, but I won't." She looked over at me as we opened our car doors. "I didn't agree not to tell, and if this helps us get closer to the truth, it'll be worth hurting Zac's feelings."

I parked my car and asked directions to Elliott's office. The golf pro answered the door on the first knock and ushered us into a homey-looking office, complete with TV, coffeemaker, microwave, and couch. Even a small refrigerator. All the comforts of home. I might have looked a bit surprised.

"Sometimes, when I have an early lesson, I sack out here the night before." He gave us a sheepish smile.

"No wonder you're not married. Or are you? I mean, were you?" Not my most shining moment.

Carly glared, but I was too far away for her to kick, so I opened my mouth, fully prepared to insert the other foot in the name of seeing justice done.

"What my sister means, Elliott, is that if you have no one at home waiting, staying overnight here would be a sensible thing to do." Then she surprised me and took the type of breath I used to take before leaping from the high board at a swim meet. "Elliott." She leveled him with one of Mama's you'd-best-come-clean-I-know-all-about-it-anyway looks. I guess when you have kids, you inherit the ability to pull off that look as needed. "Zac told us about your fiancée breaking up with you. And that you blamed Hank."

"Zac didn't mean to—" I felt like I had to defend my nephew even if his friend was a murderer.

Elliott held up his hand to stop me. "It's okay. I don't blame Zac at all. I wouldn't have spilled my sorry story to him if I'd known what was about to happen." He motioned to the couch. "Would you ladies like to sit down?"

We settled in on the sofa, and he sat across from us in a wingback recliner.

I mentally reviewed my list of questions.

Carly leaned toward Elliott. "Why did you blame Hank?"

Oh yes, question number one. We'd agreed that if he told us about the Dear Pru letter on his own, that would be a big point in his favor. What we hadn't discussed was Carly asking the questions. Suddenly I realized what was going on. In spite of my promise, she didn't trust me not to hurt Elliott's feelings, or perhaps alienate him forever.

"I don't know now." His face reddened slightly, and he looked out the window as if the answer were there.

Uh-oh. Not good. Carly obviously agreed, because she avoided my glance.

Elliott drew his gaze back to me, as if he knew that even though Carly was asking the questions, I was the one demanding answers. "My fiancée, Heather, wrote the *Monitor* and asked some advice columnist what to do." He ran his hand over his face. "Dear Pro, or something like that, told her to dump me and get on with her life. Heather left me a good-bye letter and put the advice column in the envelope with it. I'm embarrassed to admit it, but I stormed into Hank's office and threatened to sue him and his paper for interfering with my life." He shrugged. "I didn't mean it. Heather and I had been growing apart for a while. But I was so caught up in my dream of what life was supposed to be that I pushed all my doubts to the back of my mind. You know?"

Carly and I nodded.

"I was giving lessons early and late, focused on my goal of being able to afford a nice house and so forth, things I thought she wanted. But then I lost sight of the real goal. Having a life."

"That's easy to do," Carly said softly. "Sometimes I've felt that way about getting my kids grown. I concentrate so much on the end result that I lose sight of the journey."

"I can understand that," Elliott said, smiling at her. "And I imagine, with your kids, the journey is the fun part."

He obviously hadn't met the twins. But he was just as obviously besotted with my sister.

"So you didn't kill him?" Carly asked.

He jumped to his feet, towering over us. "No, Carly. Of course I didn't. But if I did, would I tell you? I understand your wanting to help Zac. But this is your plan? Ask anyone who might be involved?"

"Sort of," Carly squeaked.

Elliott sat back down, and his voice softened. "I didn't mean to scare you, but. . .that's a bad plan. Whoever killed Hank means business. The best thing you two can do is let the police handle this." He put his hand on Carly's and squeezed.

I cleared my throat and stood. "So we've been told."

Carly sat like a lump on the couch, holding hands with the suspect. I cleared my throat again, and she reluctantly pulled her hand loose and got to her feet. "Jenna thought that we should look into it on our own," Carly confessed.

Now that all the blame was on my shoulders, I decided to ask one more question. "No offense, Elliott, but where were you when Hank was killed?"

Wow. Who knew Carly could slug that hard? I'd sport a bruise on my shoulder from that.

I glared at her. "Ouch! Look, I believe you, too, Elliott. But we need some type of proof. I mean, anyone can say, 'I didn't do it.' We need to *know* you didn't."

Elliott threw back his head and laughed. "You're right, Jenna. But the police have questioned me extensively. I guess the golf club pointed them in my direction, too. If only the killer had used something like a baseball bat. Then maybe the high school coach would be the one getting all the attention."

"I know." I did feel bad for him. What if Hank had been killed with a pair of swim goggles? I could've been in Elliott's shoes.

"So you don't have an alibi?"

He shook his head. "He was apparently killed in the very early morning hours. And I don't give lessons before daylight. It's so hard to hit the golf ball in the dark."

We laughed. "Thanks for putting up with our questions. You're a good sport," I said.

"Well, that's my alibi, then. Normally, murderers are not good sports."

As we walked to the door, Elliott cleared his throat. "Carly?"

We turned.

"I don't see any need to mention this little visit to Zac, do you?"

Her smile was a little teary. "Thanks, Elliott."

"Anytime."

Friday, right after lunch, my boss walked in wearing a Hawaiian print shirt and khaki shorts. "Bob!"

"Jenna! Baby doll! It's good to see you." He held his arms out.

I gave him a side squeeze and smiled. "Good to see you, too. When did you get home?"

"Just drove in from the airport. Dropped Wilma and the luggage off at home and came over here to see what was going on." He released me and looked around the health club with a toothy grin. "Good to be home. Anything exciting happen while we were gone?"

Um, no, other than a violent murder, not a thing. But surely Wilma's sister had already told him all about that. She wasn't one to leave news left untold.

His gaze settled back on me. "That was sure too bad about old Hank, wasn't it?"

"Yes, it was." In so many ways.

"They have any idea who did it?" He walked over to the watercooler and filled a little paper cone with water, then turned back to me. "Or why?"

"I'm not sure." I leaned against the U-shaped counter. If he hadn't already heard about Zac, I wasn't about to tell him. And if he had and was fishing for more information, I certainly wasn't going to satisfy his curiosity. I pretended to be absorbed in the stretch exercise chart posted on the outside of the workstation.

"Doesn't surprise me, him getting killed. Guess he finally took a story too far, you think?" He walked around to the inside of the U and started flipping through the sign-in registry.

"I suppose that's what the police are trying to find out." No need to mention my own investigation, which, so far, wasn't doing anything but opening up more questions.

"You sent flowers from the club, right?"

"Yes. I figured you'd want me to out of sympathy for Marge and Theo." Hank had been on the zoning committee a long time. Thanks to him and a few others, Bob's dream of building his athletic club in the heart of Lake View's historic district had been squashed like a bug. He wouldn't have sent Hank flowers for his own sake.

"Well, Marge, anyway. I always heard Hank and Theo didn't get along too good."

"Really? I hadn't heard that." Okay, maybe I was getting carried away. Every seemingly innocuous statement struck me as significant.

"Yeah, I figure Hank wanted his boy to stay around here instead of gallivanting off all over the world." He held up the sheets. "So how's the club? Things pretty slow?"

What did he think? That everyone would suddenly stop working out because he was gone on a cruise?

"No, everything's been going great." Actually, if anything, we were busier than usual, but his ego was just big enough to be hurt by that coincidence, so I didn't elaborate.

"Nobody's gotten hurt or anything?" Bob always worried that someone was going to get injured at the health club and sue him. As far as I knew, no one had ever even threatened him. But go figure. Sometimes we worry the most about the things least likely to happen. And vice versa. When I started teaching, I never worried for a second that a student would die during one of my classes. But that didn't stop it from happening.

"Not so far, but you know the odds increase every year that someone will." Ooh, that was mean, playing on his fear like that. Still, he had promised me an option to purchase, and I was tired of him avoiding me.

"So the sooner you sell the place to me, the less likely you'll get sued."

He dropped the sign-in registry like it was a subpoena to court. "Well, I'd better go on home, hon. Wilma will be wondering where I've been. I'll see you tomorrow." He walked out before I could say another word. That man was seriously starting to annoy me. He avoided every mention of selling, and with nothing in writing, there was no way I could force his hand.

I slammed my fist on the granite countertop just as Byron Stanton strolled through the double glass doors. Perfect. A little casual interrogation of the mayor should use up the adrenaline left over from my nonconfrontation with Bob.

He swept through the foyer and surveyed the room like a king looking over his subjects. "Is Amelia here yet?"

Was the king speaking to me, a lowly peasant? Judging by the expectant way he was looking at me, I guessed he was. "I haven't seen her." I checked the sign-in registry. "Nope, she hasn't signed in yet."

"She's late, then. She was supposed to be here at four."

Oops. Let's throw her in the dungeon. "Why don't you have a seat in the smoothie bar and I'll get you a drink while you wait." Not my job. And I normally wouldn't make an exception for the king of Lake View, but I wasn't about to pass up the opportunity to ask him a few questions.

"Thanks." He nodded as if bestowing an honor on me.

A few minutes later, I slid a tangerine smoothie

onto his table and handed him a straw. "Mayor Stanton, I want to offer my condolences to your family. I know you and Hank weren't close, but I'm sorry for your loss." Maybe I was overdoing the sympathy here, but I wasn't sure how to start a conversation about murder with the possible murderer.

"Thanks. I'll pass that on to Amelia." Always politically correct, our mayor. I had hoped to get more of a response than that.

Maybe he needed a little more prodding. "Do the police know the motive?"

"Possibly someone was just trying to make our small town a better place to live." Byron looked over my shoulder as if this conversation was way too boring for him to give his full attention to it.

"I heard he was getting ready to write another editorial about you. Did you know that?"

"Where did you hear that?" His brown eyes flashed with irritation. I definitely had his full attention now.

"You know how things are. Word gets around."

"Jenna, it sure would be a shame if the police were to have to take your nephew down to the station again for more questioning, wouldn't it?" He smiled the coldest smile I'd ever seen.

"You don't have to get snippy. I was just curious."

"Hasn't anyone ever told you that curiosity killed the cat?"

I nodded slowly. "I've heard that." A hundred times, but no need to volunteer that information. "So if I don't butt out, you're threatening to have Zac hauled in for questioning again?" If this were a made-for-TV movie, I'd be wearing a wire. Unfortunately, it was the real world, and I just wanted to hear him say it flat out.

"Threatening? Me?" He smiled again. I wished he'd quit doing that. It seriously creeped me out. "I'm a friend, looking out for your family's reputation."

"What family's reputation are you talking about?" Amelia appeared at my shoulder, in white shorts and a T-shirt, wiping her face with the edge of a towel draped around her shoulder. How did she do that? Pop up with no warning?

I smiled sweetly. "I'll let Byron explain it to you." I spun on my heel and walked through the open area of the smoothie bar, outwardly calm, inwardly a gelatin mass. By the time I got to the doorway, Lake View's First Couple had their heads together in heated conversation. I'd stirred something up. I just had no idea what.

I was still steaming over Byron's threats when I left work that night. That might explain why I snapped at the Price Cutter cashier. Or it could have been because she was extremely annoying. I didn't know Marita very well, since she'd been several years ahead of me in school, but when she rang up my frozen pizza, Dr Pepper, and dog food, she raised her eyebrows. "Big Friday night planned?"

Many retorts danced through my head. But the one that came out was "Actually, yes." Technically that was true, since I'd already put in a call to the video store next to the grocery store and the clerk was holding a new release for me.

She scanned my single-serving pizza and clucked her tongue. "Bless your heart, sweetie. By the way, how's Zac handling all this?"

Me being dateless? I knew what she meant, so I decided to play nice. "Fine."

"Do you think he did it?"

"Of course not!"

"I don't know. Teenagers these days can be pretty unpredictable."

Unpredictable? Last time I checked, *unpredictable* was missing curfew by ten minutes occasionally. *Unpredictable* was *not* beating someone to death with a golf club. I handed her my twenty and took a deep breath. "He didn't do it."

"That's what people on television always say, isn't it? The neighbors—you know how they say, 'He was the nicest guy. He couldn't have done it.'" She ran my twenty-dollar bill over the edge of the counter to smooth it out and slipped it into her cash register. "Then they start finding the bodies under the house. . ."—she nodded over my head at Mona, the other cashier, who'd stopped to listen to Marita's tactless droning—". . .in the freezer. . ."

"Yes, I know what you mean. Happens all the time." I took my change and groceries with a sweet smile. "Some small-town grocery-store clerk turns out to be a mass murderer. Say, Marita. . .where were you the morning Hank was murdered?"

Marita's eyes widened, and she clapped her hand over her mouth. At least she wasn't talking anymore. I stomped out to my car and deposited the groceries, then strolled over to the video store.

"Hey, Jenna! I already rang up your movie." Susan laid the plastic box on the counter by the door while I paid. "You'll love it."

"You said it was a comedy, and I'm in the mood for funny. That's good enough for me." I slid my change into my pocket and grabbed the movie.

As soon as I got home, I invited Mr. Persi in to play and let Neuro out of her carrier. While I heated my pizza, they batted one of Neuro's toys around the floor. I kept one eye on the big dog and wondered at his gentle spirit. The cautious way he moved around with Neuro reminded me of a giant of a man with a little girl. He was playful but mindful of his strength.

I hate to eat alone, so I gave both animals a piece of pizza before I settled into my recliner and pushed the PLAY button on the remote control. Susan had nailed it. The movie was a riot. Small-town murder and a bumbling amateur detective. She barely escaped the killer's vengeful plots over and over without ever being aware of them. Struck a little too close to home, though, and three-quarters of the way through, I'd enjoyed all of it I could stand. Neuro was asleep on my lap and Mr. Persi on my feet. "Time for bed," I muttered.

Later, after Mr. Persi was safely tucked into the laundry room, Neuro perched on the vanity and licked her paws, watching intently as I brushed my teeth and washed my face, still thinking about the movie. "Am I as clueless as that woman?" I asked her as we padded over to the bed. I snuggled under the comforter and looked down at her where she curled up next to my feet. "I failed in the Olympics, I failed as a teacher, I can't get Bob to sell me the business, and now I can't solve Hank's murder." I raised myself up partway, punched my pillow, and then lay back down. "Trouble is, everybody seems guilty," I murmured as the world as I knew it faded into oblivion.

A crowd was gathered around the health-club receptionist's desk when I walked in. Amelia's neon-orange spandex workout clothes made me raise my hand to shade my eyes.

"There she is," she said, pointing an orange fingernail at me.

"What's wrong?" I peered over her shoulder, but the crowd blocked my view.

The man beside her turned around. Brendan Stiles, holding up a wallet. "Looking for this?" he snarled at me. How had I ever thought he was handsome?

"What are you talking about? I gave that to John."

John broke away from the group, the light off his

badge glinting in my eyes worse than Amelia's neon. He walked toward me.

"John, I'm so glad you're here. I think you should question Byron. And Elliott. Or even Brendan. One of them killed Hank."

"That's your plan, huh? Take the heat off yourself by pointing a finger at them? Why'd you do it?" John dangled a pair of handcuffs in front of him, the *clink-clink* echoing in the high-ceilinged room.

My heart thudded against my ribs. "I didn't kill Hank."

"Who said anything about Hank?" John asked, shaking his head sadly. "Zac killed him."

I gasped. "He did not!"

Behind him, Marita, the Price Cutter cashier, wagged her finger at me. "Yes, he did, sweetie. Just like I said."

"Fore!" Elliott called and pretended to line up the perfect shot down the tile hallway. He swung away with his golf club at an imaginary ball. "And she had the nerve to accuse me," he said to a man next to him. I couldn't see his face clearly, but I was afraid it was Alex.

"I didn't accuse you!"

"You accused almost everybody, trying to hide the truth, I guess." Marge, with sorrow-filled eyes, stepped toward me. "Jenna, honey, I didn't believe it. You were always such a sweet little girl. But now I know it's true."

"It's not true!" I screamed.

I opened my mouth to say more, but Marge was no longer Marge, but Marge's friend Lois, the librarian. "Shh. . .this is a library." She held her finger to her lips.

"It is not! This is the health club."

Debbie, the waitress from the diner, appeared beside her, looking bored. She peered in her hand-held mirror to apply a fresh coat of red lipstick, then smacked her lips. "Homicide must run in the family. To think I trusted you."

"Homicide? Is someone else dead?" I ran toward the crowd. What—or who—were they gathered around? John grabbed my arm.

I jerked away from him and crashed between Marita and Debbie, determined to see what they were hiding.

My pulse pounded in my throat, and I let out a low moan. My boss, Bob, in a Hawaiian shirt and khaki shorts, lay unmoving on the tile floor. My favorite swim goggles framed his unblinking eyes, and strands of thin black videotape wrapped tightly around his neck.

11

> *Lake View Monitor*
>
> The *Monitor* weather forecast
> for the Lake View area Satur-
> day: 70% chance of rain with
> thunderstorms possible. Highs
> in the mid-70s and lows in the
> upper 40s.

So he actually said that? That Zac might get taken back in for questioning?" Carly's indignation came across the phone line loud and clear.

"Would I make something like that up?" I plopped down on the couch with my coffee. I loved the health club, but weekends were definitely my favorite part of the week. Saturday mornings at home rocked. I looked out the window. Even cloudy ones.

"Oh, I hope it's him," Carly growled.

"Huh?"

"You know, the murderer. I hope it turns out to be Byron." Then she sighed. "That's not fair to Mama and Daddy, though, with the cabins and all. Nothing puts a town's tourist business in the toilet faster than the mayor being charged with murder."

I stroked Neuro's back, still grappling with the fact

that genteel Carly had said "toilet." She must be even more upset than I realized. "You're right. Let's hope it's a stranger. Someone we don't know."

"Not very likely, though, is it?"

"No, 'fraid not. And we've got to figure it out soon. You won't believe what I dreamed last night."

After I told her the morbid details of my nightmare, she laughed. "So you think you got so sick of him not selling you the business that you put your swim goggles on him and killed him with a videotape?"

"I guess. It was bizarre. But so real that when I woke up, I had to go check to be sure the tape was still where I left it."

"I told you to give up your dinosaur VCR and get a DVD player. Maybe this will convince you."

"It's doubtful. I've got too many VHS tapes to switch over now. You know how I am about change."

"Yeah, and you call John stubborn. By the way, you never told me what he said about the pills."

"*Ack.* I got so mad at him for laughing at me about the Dear Pru letter that I forgot to mention the pills. They're probably nothing anyway."

"You're right. Hang on, girl, I've got another call."

"Sure." I shoved myself to my feet and meandered into the kitchen. Mr. Persi followed me, his expression hopeful. "Hungry, boy?" I poured dog food into his dish, and he dug into it as if he hadn't been fed for a week. I could sympathize. I nuked a leftover piece of pizza and picked up my vitamin bottle. Empty.

I'd have to stop by the pharmacy and get some

more. No wonder those empty bottles at the newspaper office were from the Lake View Pharmacy. It was the most popular drugstore in town.

Suddenly the silence of a dead line was broken by a sob.

"Carly? What's wrong?"

"That was John. He wants to bring Zac back in for more questioning."

Anger shot through me. "Thanks to Byron, of course."

"I don't know." Her voice shook. "He said, 'In light of some new evidence.' What do you think that means?"

"It means our chief of police is on the mayor's payroll. But I'll take care of that. Is Zac there?" I walked back into the living room and slipped on my shoes.

"Yes."

"Okay, call Alex and have him meet us there. Do you want me to pick you and Zac up?" I snatched my keys from the hook by the door.

"No, thanks. I can drive. Besides, Daddy will want to come, too."

"Good. Let John and Byron see that we're not going to let them do this to Zac. I'm going on over. See you there."

"Okay, thanks, Jen."

I may have broken the speed limit slightly on the way to the station, but I figured the cops in our town were too busy railroading innocent sixteen-year-old boys to be worried about a little speeding. As I got out of my car, I cast a glance at the overcast sky. It wasn't our big storm season, but I felt one coming on. Maybe it was my mood.

The sergeant at the front desk opened her mouth to speak to me, but I hurried past her and made a bee-line for John's office. The door stood partially open, and that was invitation enough for me.

John looked up from his desk, and his face red-dened. "Jenna. What are you doing here?"

"What's wrong? Easier to pick on teenagers than full-grown adults? I never figured you for a coward."

He held up his hand. "Whoa. What are you talk-ing about?"

"I'm talking about our esteemed *mayor*." I spat out the word. "We both know he's the reason Zac was called in this morning."

John's brows knitted together. "Now you're con-fusing me. What does Byron have to do with this?"

"You mean besides using you to cover up the fact that he killed his brother-in-law?"

John stood. "That's a serious accusation. I think you'd better stop and take a deep breath."

I marched over to the desk, so tall in my anger that I could almost believe I towered over him instead of vice versa. "Believe me, I've had plenty of time for deep breaths ever since Byron threatened this very thing yes-terday at the health club."

"Threatened to have Zac brought in? Why would he do that?"

"His reasons are clear. He killed Hank and wants

me to stop trying to prove it. You're the one I can't figure out." I slapped my hand on the desk, and his Styrofoam cup of coffee sloshed.

"Jenna—" He retrieved his coffee cup and moved it to the windowsill. Out of the crazy woman's reach, obviously.

"Sure, we've disagreed a lot, but I thought you had integrity." Tears stung my eyes. "I can't believe you brought in an innocent teen just because I asked Byron a few questions he didn't like."

"Jenna—" John walked around the desk and reached out his hand as if to stave off an attack.

"How could you? I'm pretty sure Byron killed Hank, and here you are letting him tell you what to do."

"Stop it!" John yelled in my face. The vein in his neck bulged.

I didn't say a word. Even if he was a lowlife, if I caused him to have a stroke, Denise would kill me.

He followed his own advice and took a deep breath, then spoke softly. "Mayor Stanton didn't kill anybody."

"I think there's a good chance he did." I lowered my own voice as if the entire Lake View police station hadn't already heard our heated exchange.

"Look, I give you my word, he had nothing to do with me calling Zac in. I know you're upset and worried, but that's no excuse to go throwing accusations around. He's the mayor, for goodness' sake."

"And that means he's above the law?"

"No, and neither is your nephew. I had a reason for bringing Zac in, but it had nothing to do with the mayor."

"So I'm supposed to believe this whole thing is a funny coincidence?" I was practically foaming at the mouth now.

"Calm down and listen to me. This. Has. Nothing. To. Do. With. Mayor. Stanton." He said the words one at a time as if I were slow-witted.

"Okay then, Mr. Big Shot, tell me why. Why would you put Carly and Zac through all this?"

"Look, I know you're never going to shut up and go away unless I tell you, so you'd better keep this to yourself." He sank into his leather chair.

"Tell me." My heart pounded in my throat. I knew Zac was innocent, but I could see in John's eyes that he wasn't so sure.

He nodded for me to sit across from his desk, and I did.

"An eyewitness came forward. Someone who said they saw an old car, description matching Zac's, pulling out of the parking lot at the park. We have no choice but to ask Zac if it was him and if he was in the park that morning."

"I'm sure he wasn't. He said he was out driving around, remember?"

John nodded. "I remember. Let's hope you're right."

"So you're saying Byron Stanton didn't call you? Could he have been this Johnny-come-lately 'eyewitness'?"

"Definitely not. Byron didn't call me, and I personally

interviewed the witness." John leaned back and retrieved his coffee.

"Who was it?"

John took a sip from his cup and shook his head. "You know I can't tell you that."

"But you think they're telling the truth?" That was the reason for John's obvious doubt concerning Zac's innocence? A trustworthy witness?

"They're not involved in the case and had no reason to lie that I could see. Look, let's wait and see what Zac says, okay? I promise I'll be as easy with him as possible."

"I still think Byron probably killed Hank." I pointed at his badge. "Are you too much under his thumb to investigate the possibility?"

"Please don't say that again. I'm not under anyone's thumb. But you have to stay out of this and let us do our job."

"Well, if you do your job, I will." I pushed to my feet.

"You know who you remind me of?" John tossed the half-full Styrofoam cup into the round trash can and leveled his gaze at me. "Hank Templeton. Always asking questions, always butting into other people's business. And look how things ended for him. Is that what you want?"

A tap at the door saved me from answering what I'm sure was a rhetorical question. Sergeant Betty Riley poked her curly head in the door. "They're here, Chief." She eyed me with a mix of sympathy and concern, so I was sure who "they" were. Carly and Zac had made it to the station.

Ever the professional, John stood. "Jenna, I have to go."

"I'll wait here for you to finish." I crossed my legs and relaxed in my chair, eyeing the clear polish on my fingernails with great interest.

John glared at me. "And go through my files? I don't think so. Let me rephrase. *You* have to go."

Heat rushed up my neck and into my face. John knew me too well. "Fine." I pushed myself to my feet. "I'll wait in the hall," I said over my shoulder as I shoved the door open.

John was right behind me. "You'll—" He stopped. My dad leaned against the wall beside the bench in the hall. "Hello, Mr. Stafford."

"John." Dad nodded. "You doing okay?"

"I'm sure sorry about all this."

I looked up at him. Why hadn't he told me that?

"I know you are. You'd better get on in and do your job. Carly and Zac are in there, with Alex, of course. Jenna and I will wait out here."

"Yes, sir." John didn't even glance at me as he walked down the hallway.

Dad pulled me to him and patted my back. "You okay?"

"Just tired of all of them trying to pin this on Zac. You?"

He nodded and released me, giving me a gentle nudge toward the bench.

I sat, and he sank down beside me. "Do you know what's going on?"

I knew what John had told me, but often Daddy had an uncanny sense for the truth of the matter. "Do you?"

He smiled. "I know you've been asking questions."

I looked at him. How did he know that? I knew Carly wouldn't tell, and I hadn't told anyone else.

Behind the worry for Zac, I saw a little twinkle in his eye. He knew what I was thinking. "I heard it at the diner."

So Debbie was a tattletale. Or was it Brendan? Or Byron? Or Amelia? Or Elliott? Whew. Maybe I should slow down on the questioning or at least quit assuming that nobody knew what I was up to.

"Yeah, I've been trying to get a little information." I found myself telling him everything—except about my job as Dear Pru, since I'd only gotten permission to tell Carly and no one else.

"Sounds like you've been busy."

"So far nothing to show for it." I leaned back against the wall and closed my eyes. Here came the lecture. *Mind your own business. I don't want you to get hurt.*

"Maybe you haven't asked the right person yet."

My eyes opened, and I looked over at my dad. No lecture? "Who else would I ask?"

"Just so happens, I was at the diner the day Hank and Brendan had that argument." He stroked his chin. "Sitting in the booth right behind them."

"Really?" To think I'd been avoiding my parents

because I didn't want them to find out I was investigating. I should have been questioning them.

"I tried not to listen, but some things I couldn't help but overhear."

"Like what?"

"Mostly the same things Debbie heard. Something about a bag."

"Oh." My heart plummeted. I'd imagined breaking the case right here and now.

"But I also heard them mention the word *pills* several times."

"Pills?" Pills. Bag. The bag of empty pill bottles. I gasped. "Dad, Brendan Stiles is the murderer." I jumped to my feet. "We've got to go tell John."

"Whoa, there, sweetie." Dad reached out and touched my arm. "Sit down and let's talk."

I obeyed but shook my head. "You don't understand. Carly and I were at the newspaper in the break room," I said quickly. "For reasons too complicated to explain. And there was a bag. In the freezer. It had empty pill bottles in it from Lake View Pharmacy."

"So?"

"So it's obvious. Brendan was doing something illegal concerning medicine. Hank found out and threatened to expose him. And Brendan killed him." My heart thudded against my ribs.

"And you think if you tell John this, he'll arrest Brendan and clear Zac?"

"Yes!" Why was he acting so hesitant? Surely he wanted to clear his own grandson.

"But you've already accused Elliott to John, right?"

"Yes, but—"

"And Byron?"

"Yes."

"So what makes you think he'll believe you?"

"We'll tell him what you told me. Plus I saw the bag of pill bottles."

"What if Brendan isn't guilty?"

"He is!" How could Daddy be so calm?

He held out his hands palms up in that let's-reason-this-out manner I knew so well. "But what if he and Hank were arguing over some ad copy and whether or not to use certain pictures with it? And what if Brendan was saying, 'I gave you that bag of empty pill bottles so you could get some good shots for the ad, and now you're not going to use them?' "

I leaned against the wall again. "Do you think that was what they were talking about?"

"No. But I'm still not convinced Brendan killed him. And I'd think twice before I accused another possibly innocent man."

The door to the interrogation room burst open and Zac walked out. He looked at Dad and me for a second—unreadable emotions in his red-rimmed eyes—then stomped down the hall. We rose to our feet as Carly came out next, Alex right behind her. "Hey, guys, I've got to go talk to Zac." She looked at Alex grimly. "Would you fill them in?"

"What's wrong?" I asked, icy ribbons of fear braiding around my heart.

"Zac didn't tell us the whole truth about the morning Hank was killed."

Dad shook his head. "I could tell he was hiding something."

I remembered having that feeling, too, the first day Zac had told us about being fired, that all wasn't being said. "What was it?"

Alex glanced around the deserted hallway and lowered his voice. "When he told us he was driving around that morning, he neglected to tell us that he pulled into the Main Street Park parking lot for a few minutes, then left."

"Oh no," I whispered. "What are they going to do?"

"John reminded him again not to leave town. But between us, I think if something else doesn't break in the next few days, they'll arrest him. I got the impression the DA may very well be preparing a case." He looked from Dad to me. "I'm sorry."

I hit my fist against the wall and turned to Dad. "Meet me in the car, okay? I'm going to talk to John."

Dad reached toward me then dropped his hand. "You have to do what you have to do. But remember what I said."

I nodded. "I'll be cool."

"That'll be the day," I heard Alex mutter as I walked toward the interrogation-room door. I considered going back and giving him a piece of my mind, talking about me that way and especially to my own father. But I had to deal with John first.

The Lake View Police Department's interrogation room served as a break room when there were no dangerous criminals to question. So I wasn't surprised to find John scarfing down a doughnut and coffee. When he saw me, he picked up a napkin and started wiping at his sticky fingers. "Jenna," he mumbled around the remains of his pastry.

"You've got the wrong guy. I think Brendan Stiles killed Hank."

John swallowed quickly and choked. When he didn't quit coughing, I began to beat him on the back, but he held up his hand for me to stop. "Enough."

"I'm sorry. I was only trying to help." I waited patiently while he took a big gulp of coffee.

"That's your problem," he croaked. "Always trying to help. You come in here accusing everyone and his brother of murder. Next you'll be thinking it was me."

"But I have proof that Brendan and Hank weren't getting along—"

"Hank didn't get along with anyone. Can't you get that through your head?" John threw his coffee cup in the trash and closed the doughnut box, then hurried from the room without a backward glance at me.

I guess I'd ruined his appetite. Well, pardon me. I followed him out of the room and stood in the hallway, watching his back disappear around the corner. "I'm trying to tell you who the murderer is. Can't you get that through your head?"

When I walked out of the station, I looked up at the dark clouds and a drop of rain hit me in the eye. I sprinted for my car but couldn't outrun the downpour. Lightning streaked across the sky as I jumped, soaking wet, into the driver's seat and nodded to my dad. I should have stayed home in my warm, dry pajamas.

12

Lake View Monitor

THANK YOU

The family of Hank Templeton
would like to thank everyone for their food, flowers,
prayers, and expressions of
sympathy. May God bless each
of you.

After Saturday's storms, Sunday morning in Lake View dawned bright and sunny. As I drove to church, I couldn't help but notice how full of promise the day seemed, the trees resplendent in their freshly washed, multicolored ponchos. After Alex's prediction that Zac might be arrested, I don't know what I'd expected. Maybe for the world to change overnight to grays and blacks, a dreary winter scene, more fitting to my family's mood. Instead, the changing leaves, Lake View's claim to fame, were at their most glorious. Unfortunately, the town was so abuzz with talk of murder and suspects, nobody noticed.

I had a couple of questions to ask Marge Templeton after services. Speed was essential if we wanted to save Zac the embarrassment of a false arrest, not to mention the anguish of a false conviction. But the way I looked at it, if we didn't take time out for the Lord, how could we expect Him to take time out for us?

Before I walked into the whitewashed building, I sent up a little prayer that He would help me to keep my mind on Him alone until worship was over. And when Alex squeezed in next to me right before we started, I repeated the silent petition more fervently.

Before we dismissed, Jack Thompson stood to recap the announcements. I shifted on the padded pew and allowed myself to look at Alex, clean-shaven and sharp in a gray suit. I'd studiously concentrated on forgetting he was there during the worship and had almost succeeded. But technically, announcements weren't worship.

Was it by pure accident that Alex had ended up beside me this morning? Or had he sought me out? Maybe with the new threat, since he was Zac's lawyer, he thought he should sit with the family. But Mama and Daddy were at the other end of the bench, and he'd have shown just as much support down there. Not that I was complaining.

Jack's last announcement pulled my attention to the front. "Oh, by the way, we're glad to have Marge Templeton back with us today. She asked me to thank you all for the food and prayers. Your dishes will be on a table in the fellowship hall."

I watched heads turn toward an area on the opposite side of the building. I'd have to hurry to get over to Marge before she left.

After the closing prayer, Alex turned to me, his smile crinkling the corners of his eyes. "Jenna, how's it going?"

"Fine." I watched Marge's permed curls bounce down the aisle toward the front of the building. *She must be getting the dishes from her car to take to the fellowship hall.* I looked back at Alex. "How are you?"

His smile was a shade less bright. "I'm okay. You looking for someone?"

"Me? No." Not anymore.

"I was wondering if you have plans for lunch?"

"I usually go over to Mama's on Sundays. Um. . ." Marge had left the building. If I let this chance to talk to her go by, who knew when I'd get another one that didn't feel forced? I felt a trickle of perspiration at the back of my neck.

I wanted to go out with Alex, but was I ready to open that Pandora's box and poke and prod at all the old hurts there? I turned to Carly, who was sitting on the other side of me. Her normally smooth face was drawn with worry. "Carly. Talk to Alex for a minute." I stepped deftly out into the aisle, leaving them facing each other looking puzzled. "We'll talk later, okay? I have to see someone. I'll be back!" I called.

Had I flipped my lid? Judging by the openmouthed look Alex gave me, he sure thought so. I'd have to worry about that later.

I speed-walked down the aisle, because one of Mama's firmest childhood rules had concerned running in the church building. And she might be looking. I reached the fellowship hall as Marge set the dishes on the table. I glanced at the doorway to the tiny kitchen but saw no one. Perfect. "Marge."

She spun around. "Jenna, honey. So good to see you."

I hugged her. "You, too."

"Did you come to get your bowl?" She reached for my bowl, and I took it and set it on the table in front of me.

"Thanks." I had my carefully rehearsed speech prepared. Lead with a couple of questions about Dear Pru and then ease into some delicate questions about Hank and the empty pill bottles we found at the newspaper office. Contrary to my reputation at the diner, I could be subtle. Deep breath. "Actually, I wanted to see how you were doing and ask your advice about the Dear P—"

"Lois is in the kitchen, washing up a few things. Do you want me to ask her for a bag for you to put your bowl in?" Marge actually wiggled her eyebrows and put her finger to her lips in a shushing motion.

"Um, okay. Sure." I guess she wasn't exaggerating about keeping the Dear Pru identity a secret, if even her best friend was kept in the dark. So much for my lead-in to the real questions.

Without waiting to be asked, Lois bustled out with a plastic grocery bag and handed it to me.

"Here," Marge said, taking the bag from me, "let me do it."

"Oh, thanks." I relinquished the bag, wondering how to bring up the pills.

I never thought I would be grateful to be the subject of gossip, but when Marge said, "I was over at Shear Joy for my weekly set yesterday, and Joyce said you had an argument with that boyfriend of yours at the bowling alley the other night." I'd have kissed the garrulous beautician if she had been there.

"Well, he isn't actually my boyfriend, but yes, we had a small tiff. Speaking of Brendan, do you know if Hank was doing any kind of investigation of him or the pharmacy?"

"I have no idea. Why do you ask?" Marge was still wrestling the bowl into the plastic bag, but her furrowed brow and pursed lips clearly said, *I'll handle this,* so I left her alone.

"What have you heard?" Lois leaned forward, obviously eager to hear the latest gossip. Guess she wanted to contribute her share at the beauty shop or pass along a little extracurricular knowledge at the library.

"Nothing specific, you know; you just pick up things here and there." Like empty pill bottles in freezers.

"If he was investigating, he didn't mention it to me," Marge said, finally getting the bowl in the bag.

"Well, do either of you know Anne Mansfield or Josephine Winston?"

Marge was handing me the bowl, tied up neatly in a plastic bag, but before I could loop my hands through the handles, it slipped from her hands and shattered on the floor.

"Oh, Jenna, I'm so sorry." Tears filled Marge's eyes, and she squatted down to scoop up the bag of broken glass.

"There, there, dear. Jenna knows it was an accident." Lois patted her friend's shoulder. She pulled a tissue from her purse and handed it to Marge.

"Don't worry about it. Honestly. It was a bargain-aisle special." I took the bag and tossed it into the trash can beside us. "At least it was all bagged up so we don't have to get the broom, right?" Marge looked unconvinced, so I figured I might as well press on. "Anyway, where were we? Oh yeah, Anne Mansfield? Josephine Winston?"

Lois tapped her lips with her fingertip. "Those names don't sound familiar to me at all. Do they to you, Marge?"

Marge swiped a tear away and arranged the dishes on the table to fill in the spot left vacant by my bowl. "No," she said thoughtfully, "but you know, our small town is growing so fast, all those big-city people moving to the country." She sounded depressed by the idea.

"I heard the other day that Harvey and Alice were thinking of putting the diner up for sale. I bet they won't have any trouble selling it." Lois was back to her gossip again.

By the time I finished talking to them, Alex was long gone. I couldn't decide if I was relieved or disappointed, but the heavy feeling in my chest didn't feel much like relief. I was almost to Mama and Daddy's before I realized that neither of the ladies had even asked why I wanted to know about Anne Mansfield and Josephine Winston.

I parked around back at Mama's and went in the

kitchen door. When Carly was upset, nothing could keep her from cooking. Not even the fact that she was still wearing her Sunday dress.

"Where've you been?" Carly asked from the stove as she stirred a pot of something that smelled delicious. Mama's old KISS THE COOK apron was draped around her dress. "And what was with the disappearing act?"

"I had to talk to Marge." I looked around the empty kitchen and lowered my voice anyway. "I wanted to find out if she knew who those women were whose names were on the bottles."

"Did she?" Carly slid open the drawer, retrieved a teaspoon, and bumped the drawer shut with her hip. She dipped it in the pan and held the spoon of tomatoey-looking liquid up to me. "Taste this."

"She had no idea. Neither did Lois." I blew the spoonful gently, then drank it down. "Yum. Your spaghetti sauce is always perfect."

"Thanks. Bummer about the pills. Drain that spaghetti for me, if you don't mind."

I stretched on tiptoes and retrieved the strainer from the top shelf of the cabinet. "Where's Mama?"

"She and the girls are changing out of their church clothes."

"But you couldn't be bothered, right?"

Her wry grin didn't reach her eyes. "I had to get my mind off things."

"Daddy and Zac in the living room, I guess?"

"Mm-hmm." She sprinkled a little more garlic powder in the sauce.

"How's Zac holding up?"

"He's wishing he'd turned around somewhere else that morning rather than the Main Street Park driveway. Still, I don't think he thought it was a big deal not mentioning it the first time he was questioned. So he's pretty stunned. But he's counting on God and Alex to get him out of this mess."

"Speaking of Alex, what happened with him after I left?" I'd given her every opportunity to volunteer the information, but since she hadn't, I decided I'd ask.

"Daddy came over and invited him to come over for lunch. Bless his heart, I could tell he didn't know what to say after you ran off like that. Then Mama wandered over and invited him, too. Poor Alex stammered all over the place before he finally got out of lunch."

"Poor Alex? Whose side are you on anyway?"

"Side? Who said anything about sides? I thought you were enjoying seeing him again."

"I was at first. But he's taken his slow, sweet time about asking me out, don't you think?" An invitation extended to both Carly and me to go eat after Hank's funeral did *not* count. Nor did his agreeing to go play golf with us last Saturday.

"So you're pouting?"

Why'd she have to make it sound like that? "Let's just say that his hesitation has made me realize that I shouldn't jump into anything, either." I ran water over the noodles. "I don't want to get hurt again."

"Maybe he doesn't, either." She took the spaghetti

from me and dumped it into a glass casserole dish. In seconds, she'd poured the sauce in, stirred it together, sprinkled the whole thing with Colby Jack cheese, and popped it into the preheated oven.

"I'm not the one who left town twelve years ago."

"Yeah, but you said he tried to call and you wouldn't talk to him."

"Oh, well," I huffed. "If he gives up that easy, I don't know how he ever made it through law school."

"And you say you never hold a grudge." She tsk-tsked me as she brushed butter on top of the rolls she'd made earlier.

The door from the living room swished open just as Carly said that, and Mama smiled a welcome at me. When we were growing up, we watched the Waltons, and Mama always reminded me of Olivia Walton. Her smile was as gracious as her voice was soft. "Hi, honey, glad you made it. Who's holding grudges in my kitchen?" Yet, like Olivia, she always managed her house, especially the kitchen, with a firm hand.

"Thanks," I mumbled to Carly. "Nobody, Mama. Carly's teasing."

"Oh, good." Mama bustled over to put the tea-kettle on to boil. Neither Carly nor I dared to make tea with Mama around. She's the master of sweet tea, and our family would tolerate nothing of lesser quality. "Hand me those tea bags, please."

I retrieved the box from the counter and passed it over to her. "Speaking of grudges, though, Mama, do you know why Hank and Byron fought all these years?

Are they the only reason Marge and Amelia don't get along?"

"Hmm, I don't guess I know the specific thing that made them fight. If there was one. As far as Marge and Amelia, when their family first moved to Lake View, they were as thick as thieves. The sisters and Lois. Three beautiful girls—always together." She measured a liberal portion of sugar into the bottom of her tea pitcher. "Then not too long after I met them, something tore the sisters apart. I never did know what."

"I didn't know Lois was from here." Carly checked the broccoli with a fork.

"She moved here with their family after her dad died in a fire, sort of a foster daughter, I think."

"No wonder she always tries to help Marge out. You think Amelia got jealous of their friendship?"

Mama seemed to consider this, then shook her head. "The men came in the picture about then. More likely it had something to do with them. There's been bad blood between Hank and Byron right from the beginning. I always figured it was because each was afraid the other would get more of the family money."

I leaned against the counter and breathed in the aroma of baked spaghetti and fresh rolls. Smells that made me think of Carly and always would. Did Amelia think of Marge when she smelled spearmint? And maybe Marge remembered Amelia when she smelled. . .tanning lotion? I couldn't imagine anything ever coming between Carly and me. Certainly not money. The sisters' estrangement was almost as big a mystery as Hank's murder. At least

Zac wasn't being blamed for that one.

After lunch, the dishes were cleared, Zac took off for the golf course, and Mama asked the girls to go help her change the linens in the cabins to get ready for new guests. Carly and I offered to help, but Mama had that train-up-a-child look in her eye, so we finished up in the kitchen instead. When everything was done and Dad was snoring in his recliner, Carly tiptoed in and got the paper, then ran back into the kitchen with it, grinning as if she'd completed a secret mission. Today was my Dear Prudence debut.

She flipped it open and began to read, " 'Dear Pru, I will be sixteen in two months and twenty-three days. My parents always told me I could date when I turned sixteen. Well, I met this neat guy and he asked me out, but my mom said no. I have begged and threatened, but she won't change her mind. I am very mature and have never given my parents any reason to doubt me, so why are they sticking to this dumb rule? I mean, what difference does two months make? Sixteen is just a number. So what can I say to make them see how silly they are being? Trapped Teen.' "

"Here's the scary part," I said, leaning against her chair. "My answer."

" 'Dear Trapped, you have begged and threatened? But you are mature? Sounds to me like your mom needs to extend the no-dating rule and give you a good dictionary. When you discover the real meaning of *mature*, you will understand why they don't think you are ready. Also, it might help if you don't refer to rules made by the rule-makers (in this case, parents) as "dumb" if you want them on your side. My advice to you is simple: Grow up.' "

She laughed and clapped her hands. "Jenna, you're a natural at this."

"Do you think it was okay?" The sense of responsibility I felt answering the letters had surprised me.

"Perfect." Carly had moved on to the next letter, one from a woman who started out asking advice about how she could convince her longtime boyfriend to propose, but who ended by saying, " 'Now that I have read my own letter, I see that he's not all that great anyway. So I don't care if he proposes or not—because I'm going to dump him. Thank you, Dear Pru, for helping me see what I need to do.' Signed, 'So Over Him.' "

I nodded. If only they were all that easy.

" 'Dear So Over Him,' " Carly continued to read, laughing. " 'You're welcome!' " She looked up at me. "You did great!"

"Yeah, but look at my life. Don't you think it's kind of silly for me to be giving advice?"

"Sugar, people need to know someone cares. Look at what you've already done for Zac—"

"You mean nothing?" I dodged as she elbowed in my general direction. "Well, nothing that has helped."

"I have a feeling it will. I know I was against it, but right now, knowing you're on the case—"

"*We're* on the case." I couldn't believe she was finally coming around.

She rolled her eyes. "Whatever you want to think.

Anyway, knowing that you won't give up is the only thing keeping me from going nuts. And it proves you care. Which was my point."

I thought of Zac. He'd barely spoken at all today. Everyone else had tried to be cheerful, but even the twins seemed to know it was an act. How could I possibly give up?

13

Lake View Monitor

Dear Pru,
    I broke up with my boy-
friend and now I regret it.
I've tried to tell him, but
he won't take my calls. What
should I do?

                    ~Desperate

Alex, Jenna again. Give me a call when you get this."
I slapped my phone shut and climbed out of my car. I'd been phoning Alex for two days to apologize for leaving him so suddenly after church Sunday. Apparently he wasn't ready to accept my apology.

And as if that weren't bad enough, Carly had forgotten all about our standing Tuesday night date at the creepy deserted *Monitor* building and had already promised the twins a movie. So here I was alone. At least the hallway light stayed on permanently.

In Hank's office I turned on the overhead light and quickly retrieved the new envelopes from the Dear Pru file. I placed my typewritten copy of this week's column in the manila folder. "No way I'm going to look around without Carly to back me up. I'm outta here,"

I muttered. I turned off Hank's light and started down the hallway. A noise on the opposite side of the building froze me in my tracks.

Every side of the *Monitor* office had an exit. I'd come in the back door. But the noise came from the east side. Nothing over there but the alley that wrapped around the building. Except the central-heating unit. *The heater. . .it was the heater,* I repeated to myself silently.

A doorknob rattled in the distance. Not the heater. Someone was obviously trying to get in. An employee who'd forgotten something, maybe. Or a murderer come back to tie up some loose ends. *Should I call 911? Run for my car?* I looked up at the WOMEN sign on the wall beside me. Hide in the bathroom? If I didn't calm down, I'd need to be near the bathroom.

I heard the door open before I could decide, so I quickly slipped into the ladies' restroom. After a minute of no noise, I stuck my head out the door and looked both ways down the hall. No one in sight. But with several empty offices on both sides of the hall, that didn't necessarily mean I was alone in the building. I ducked back inside and waited, back against the wall. I could hear a muffled sound, possibly footsteps. But they didn't sound really close. I stuck my head out the door again. Nose to nose with Brendan Stiles's shocked face.

I screamed, a short frantic cry, cut off by clapping my own hand over my mouth.

"Jenna, what on earth are you doing here?" Brendan's eyes were wide and his breathing shallow. I could tell he'd considered screaming.

"I work here. What are *you* doing here?" I tried to sound normal, but my voice trembled.

"Just looking for some papers I left with Hank." He held up a key. "A buddy loaned me his key so I could get them. So you work here. What are you, the night watchman?"

"Uh. I, uh. . ." I looked down at the manila envelope still clutched in my hands. It didn't say DEAR PRU anywhere on it, thankfully. "I got a part-time clerical job here. Marge hired me." *Whew. Almost forgot my cover story.* "Why did you say you were here?" I tried for casual, hoping he'd attribute the slight quiver in my voice to leftover surprise.

"I was getting advice on some investments from Hank not too long before he died, and I left some papers with him. Since they were confidential, I wanted to pick them up before anyone else read them." He gave me that wide grin that used to make me feel like I must be wrong about his personality. I've always been a sucker for a nice smile. And his was definitely above average. But after that night at the bowling alley, I was grin-resistant.

"Thought you said you weren't friends."

"Hank was a good investor. I didn't have to be his friend to ask for his advice." The smile stayed in place, but his eyes were cold.

Uh-oh. Time to back off. "Gotcha. Well, I hope you found them. Or do you want me to help you look?" My turn to force a smile.

"No, Jenna, that's okay. I'll go look around some

more in Hank's office." He appeared to buy my helpful attitude. "There is one thing I'd like you to do, though."

"What is that?"

"I'd rather you didn't mention to anyone else that I was here." Brendan winked at me, and I forced myself not to shudder. "I don't want anyone else to know Hank was looking into those investments for me."

"Right. No one else needs to know." Except maybe John and Marge. But this was not the time to mention that. Who wanted to antagonize a killer? I just wanted out of there alive.

"So you were at the paper last night doing some clerical job for Marge. . ." John regarded me with a skeptical expression I was getting too used to seeing on his face. "And your old boyfriend dropped by. And now you want me to arrest him. Is that about it?"

"Not even remotely close. In the first place"—I held up my fingers and counted one off with the other hand—"he's not my old boyfriend. Second, he didn't know I was there when he dropped by; he was looking for some papers that he'd given Hank."

"So he broke in and you didn't call the police?"

"He had a key."

"Hmm. . ." John shook his head. "Sounds like he had as much right to be there as you did, then."

"Did I tell you about the pill bottles?"

"What pill bottles?"

"The ones in the freezer at the *Monitor*."

A different look came in his eyes. The same expression he'd worn that day I was rattling on about the wallet. "No, you didn't mention that. What about it?"

Suddenly I knew that the police had found the brown paper bag in the freezer and left it there as unimportant. "You saw them, didn't you?"

"What I saw and didn't see is none of your business, Jenna." He thumped his desk with his fist. "This case doesn't involve you."

"Really?"

"Yes, really."

"Tell that to my nephew next time you bring him down here to the station."

The desk sergeant's voice blared over the intercom. "Chief Conner, you have a phone call on line 1."

John reached for the phone then looked at me pointedly.

I plucked a peppermint from a bowl on his desk and popped it into my mouth. "I'm leaving, I'm leaving."

As I climbed into my car, I instinctively looked over at the empty passenger seat. Normally on my way to work, Neuro was there, peeking out at me from her carrier. But today Mr. Persi had balked at going outside and Neuro had actually run the other way when I opened the carrier. I'd given in and left them alone in the house. We'd see if I ended up regretting it. Slowly, I was learning to take chances on commitment.

I picked up my cell phone and dialed Alex's office.

Even though he hadn't returned my calls to his cell from yesterday, I still felt I owed him an apology.

"Tracey? This is Jenna Stafford. Do you think I could talk to Alex for a minute?"

"Sure, Jenna. I'll put you right through."

Surprise, surprise. Why hadn't I thought of phoning his office yesterday instead of wasting time calling his cell phone?

"Alex Campbell here."

His voice made my knees go weak, even over the telephone, and even though I was sitting down already. Not fair.

"Hi, it's Jenna."

"Hey, great to hear from you. What's going on in your corner of town today?"

Okay, too smooth. Besides the fact that I'd been calling and calling him? "Did you get my messages?"

"Messages?"

"On your cell phone?"

"Oh. No."

"You didn't get the messages I left you on your voice mail?"

"No, I haven't checked my messages."

Would it hurt him to expand a little? He didn't have to listen to a message to see on his caller ID that I'd called. He sounded terribly guilty, but why? "I was calling to apologize for Sunday after church. There's no excuse for how I acted, but I was trying to figure out some stuff about Hank's murder. I'm sorry."

"I accept your apology. How's your undercover investigation going?"

"Nothing so far."

"Be careful that you don't mess things up for the police."

"Have you been talking to John?" I gripped the phone tightly.

"No. . ." His voice was puzzled. "I'd just hate to see you tamper with the evidence or anything."

"I'd never do that." Unless finding the pill bottles from the *Monitor* and writing down the names on them counted as tampering.

"I know. Sorry for sounding lawyerly."

I laughed. "That's okay. It's your job. Well, I wanted to say again, I'm sorry."

Silence. Then he cleared his throat. "Thanks for calling."

"And if you'd still like to go out, that would be great." Where had that come from? I was just being a good Christian, calling to apologize to someone I'd offended. That surely didn't include soliciting a date. Besides, what if he said no?

"How about supper tomorrow night?"

Wow. An invitation for a Thursday night date. Unfortunately, I couldn't go, but Mama always said it's a sure sign a man likes you if he doesn't wait for the weekend to ask you out. "I'd love to, but I have to work late tomorrow night. How about Friday?" Unless he asked me out for Thursday night because he had a real date on Friday night? *Argh.* I had to quit second-guessing myself.

"Great! Dinner and a movie?"

"How about dinner and a walk along the river?" I guess my regular confrontations with John were making me pushy. But I'd missed Alex, and if we were going to do this, why sit in a darkened theater beside each other when we could spend that same time talking and getting to know each other again?

"Sounds even better. We've got a lot of catching up to do."

I hung up the phone, glad to have the apology off my chest and even gladder to have a real, honest-to-goodness date with Alex.

Bob came in three hours late, as he'd done every day since he got home last Friday. I only knew he was there because I saw him running on the treadmill when I walked by. Must be trying to lose the ten pounds he'd gained on the cruise. Whatever the reason, he didn't grace the office with his presence. We were going to have to have it out. But right now I had my hands full with life-or-death questions. I couldn't worry about silly little future-deciding questions.

I got off at four and didn't even try to find Bob. Instead, I flipped open my phone and called Carly. "Well, I called Alex and apologized for running off to talk to Marge on Sunday."

"I'm proud of you. Was he nice about it?" I nodded my head and realized she couldn't see me. "Well, he did act a little odd about my messages. I can't figure out why he ignored them."

I pushed the UNLOCK button on my key fob then slid into the driver's seat. A white envelope flapped against the windshield. "Hang on, Carly. There's something under my windshield wiper."

"Okay."

I clambered back out of the car and snatched the offending item. "I don't know who advertisers think they're going to impress. I know I'm dying to get out of my car after I'm already settled in."

"Who left it?"

Warm and comfortable again, I examined my find. "No idea. It's not an ad, though. Has my name on it." I ripped the envelope open and stared at the white card. "Carly," I whispered. "You won't believe this."

"What?"

I hit the Lock button on the door. Letters, all different shapes and sizes, had been cut out of a magazine and pasted onto a plain white card. Butt Out Before You Get Hurt. I started the car and glanced around the deserted parking lot. Several vehicles, but not a person in sight.

I quickly conveyed the message to Carly.

"Are you sure it's for you?"

My hand trembled as I retrieved the envelope from the passenger seat. "It says Jenna right here on the envelope."

"Oh."

"Come on. I need a little sisterly reassurance." I tried to laugh as I put the car in gear. "You can do better than that."

"Are you by yourself in the parking lot?"

"Oh, see? That's so much better. Yes. But I'm getting

out of here as quickly as I can." The motor revved as I pulled onto the road.

"Where are you going?"

"Home. I let Neuro stay home with Mr. Persi today. They're both inside. I don't think I have a choice."

"Maybe it's a good thing you have a dog now." Carly had teased me mercilessly about Miss Never Commit ending up with two pets. "Aren't you afraid someone might be waiting there for you?"

"I wasn't." I slowed down.

"Oh, sorry. Want me to meet you there?"

"Oh yeah, I can see the headline now. STAFFORD SISTERS SINGLE-HANDEDLY SUBDUE SUSPECT."

"Very funny. Seriously, though. I'll come on over right now."

"Thanks, but I'll swing by John's office and show him the note. Give him the thrill of having not just one but two visits from me in a day."

"Then what?"

"Then I'll go home."

"Alone?"

She didn't know when to quit, did she? Maybe I should name her Ms. Persistence.

"I'll call you when I leave the station, and you can meet me at the house." I slowed down at the city-limit sign. The last thing I needed was a police escort to the station.

"Good. I might get Zac or Dad to come with me."

"And mess up our headline with its perfect alliteration? We're the Stafford sisters. We can handle it."

Ten minutes later, I walked into John's office, my shoulders back and my head high. I had a legitimate reason to be here. Let him try to throw me out this time.

"What are you doing here?"

I slapped the paper down on his desk and smoothed it out with my hand, then stood back.

John studied it for a second; then his dark eyes flashed to my face. "Where'd you get this?"

"My windshield. At the health club." I produced the envelope bearing my name and put it beside the letter.

He rubbed the stubble on his chin. "Did you ever think about doing what it says?"

"I get a threatening letter with a killer on the loose and you think this is an appropriate time to chide me about minding my own business?" My voice squeaked, and I took a deep breath.

"No, I'm going to investigate it, but in the meantime I think it's real good advice."

"You're going to investigate it?" I asked, trying not to screech. "The same way you've been investigating Hank's murder. I've tried to tell you—"

He jumped to his feet. "Tried to tell me? Tried to tell me that the mayor is the murderer, or wait." He put his hand on one hip and tapped his lips with his finger in an exaggerated feminine motion. "Is it the golf pro? No, no, that's not right. It's the local pharmacist."

"Well, maybe if you listened once in a while instead of making fun of me. . ."

He yanked up the letter he'd been so careful not to touch a minute before. "Did you do this?"

"What?" Could he be saying what it sounded like?

"Did you make up this letter to throw me off Zac's trail?"

"Did you kill Hank Templeton?" I knew he didn't, but it was no more ridiculous than his accusation of me. Fury rolled like a ball in my stomach.

"Get out." He pointed his finger to the door. "Jenna Stafford, I love you like a sister, but you've crossed the line from annoying to downright interfering with my investigation. I wouldn't believe you if you had a taped confession!" The vein in his neck was bulging again.

"But I—"

"The boy that cried wolf."

"Excuse me?"

"That's what you remind me of—the boy that cried wolf." He hitched up his pants by the belt loop. "So don't come crying to me anymore."

I spun on my heel and left without a word, hoping to get out before he saw the tears streaming down my cheeks. Being unjustly accused always made me cry.

John needn't worry.

I would never call on Lake View's finest again.

Carly and Zac were waiting in her van when I pulled into my driveway. I didn't for one second think someone was in my house, but it was ironic to see my nephew motion Carly and me to get behind him as he led the way with a baseball bat clutched in his hands. How quickly boys go from being the protected to being the protector.

As soon as Zac opened the door, Mr. Persi bounded

toward us, wagging all over. Neuro hung back, in that way cats have, but I could tell she wasn't agitated. "It's all clear," I assured my nephew and took the Louisville Slugger from his hands. "Thanks."

"Cool dog." Zac scratched the dog behind his ears. "Aren't you, buddy?"

The golden retriever grunted.

"He agrees with you," Carly said.

I looked at the house—exactly as it was when I'd left it that morning. "I do, too." I patted Mr. Persi and scooped up Neuro. "Wanna take him out back, Zac?"

"Sure."

After they went out, Carly looked up at me. "You goin' to be okay?"

"I guess. Nothing a cup of hot chocolate won't cure, maybe." We sat at my bar and sipped our cocoa while I told her about my visit to the police station.

"I'm goin' over there and give him a piece of my mind." Carly's knuckles were white as she gripped my Krispy Kreme mug handle.

"You can't. That would only make things worse for Zac." We both watched out the kitchen window as the golden dog jumped to catch the Frisbee. Zac threw back his head and laughed.

Carly's eyes glistened with tears. "It's not fair."

I reached over and took her hand. "We both learned that a long time ago, Car. C'mon, who needs the police? With God's help, we can do it."

"I guess you're right, but it frustrates me to no end how pigheaded John's being." She waved her hand toward the window. "Do you think he sincerely believes that boy killed somebody?"

"I have no idea what he believes anymore." I finished my cocoa and put my cup in the sink. When she handed me hers, I sat it beside mine and nodded toward the back door. "Let's go out and play." She needed some serious downtime, and maybe it would help me to quit gritting my teeth—something I'd noticed myself doing ever since I left the station.

"Does this mean you're going through your second childhood?"

"Hey, you're older than me. Always will be," I taunted as we hurried outside.

"Aunt Jenna, catch!" Zac spun the flying disc toward me. I reached up to grab it, but a golden blur leaped into the air and intercepted it.

Zac's dimples flashed. "Can you believe how good he is?"

I took the soggy Frisbee from Mr. Persi and had a sudden flashback to retrieving Hank's wallet from him that fateful Friday morning. All roads led to the murder these days.

I tossed it to Zac. "He's got talent, that's for sure."

"Anybody ever answer your ad about him?"

I shook my head. "The vet said most likely his owner had died or ended up in a nursing home and the family just let him go. Or someone got tired of feeding him and dropped him off at the park. But I'm still not sure why he adopted me."

"He knew a good thing when he saw it." Carly

sank down on the yellow grass.

"Yeah," Zac said and draped his arm across my shoulders. "After all, you're my favorite aunt."

"Wonder why." We'd had the favorite-aunt, favorite-nephew thing going since Zac was tiny. "Maybe because I'm the only one," I growled and tickled his ribs through his T-shirt.

He ducked away from me. "Hey! I'm too old to tickle."

"That's a surefire way to know someone's not 'too old' for something," Carly drawled from the grass. "When they feel like they have to say they are."

Zac laughed. "Yeah, well. . .I don't think that made any sense, Mom." He threw the Frisbee to her, and it landed in her lap. He nodded toward Mr. Persi. "Wanna take him to the park for a while? We could go by and get the pipsqueaks."

"Sure."

"Sounds good. I'm sure Hayley and Rachel will be thrilled," Carly agreed and reached out a hand for Zac to help her up. "Since when do you want to go to the park with your family?"

Zac winked at me as he tugged his mama to her feet. "Since my aunt got a dog that's cool enough to be a chick magnet." He opened the door. "Come on, Mr. Persi—" He froze and looked over his shoulder at me. "Any chance he's up for a name change? 'Mr. Persi' is kinda weird-sounding."

It was so good to see Zac acting more like his old self. Maybe if we could clear his name, he wouldn't have any lasting scars from this ordeal. "You're more than welcome to call him by his full name—Mr. Persistence."

"Ooo-kay. Maybe I'll stick with 'Hey, dog.' "

Sadly enough, "Hey, dog" followed him into the house without complaint and stuck right to his side the rest of the afternoon.

I clutched the intercom mic and made the announcement I make every Thursday night at 7:40. "Lake View Athletic Club will be closing in twenty minutes." One of the first improvements I made when I started working here, the announcement cut down on closing time.

"Night, Jenna!" Dave called. "Sure you don't want me to wait and walk you out to your car?"

"I'm sure." The personal trainer asked the same thing every week, but so far I'd managed to steer clear of Mr. Universe. The endless parade of blonds on his arm anytime I saw him after hours gave a pretty clear indication this was not a man who might help me meet my deadline. And I tried not to listen to locker room talk, but apparently when he was with the guys, he never shut up bragging about his conquests. He was cute, but I wasn't about to be another notch in his barbell.

"Night, Jenna. Everyone's cleared out of the locker rooms. Want me to wait on you?" Gail asked. She had her hands full with her college load and her job here, so sometimes she was kind of scattered, but she was a big help to me. And the members loved her.

"No, thanks, Gail. I'll be right behind you."

I flipped off the last light switch and let the door *whoosh* shut behind me, then stood with my key in the doorknob as I went over my mental checklist. Had I checked the pool area and all locker rooms to make sure there were no stragglers? With Gail's help, yes. Had I checked the coffeepot and smoothie-bar area to make sure everything was turned off? Yes. Had I set the security alarm before shutting the door? Yes.

Satisfied, I locked the door. It seemed darker than normal tonight. *Must be a new moon. Or maybe just my nerves.* As I was walking across the deserted parking lot, Carly's nagging advice about making someone stay late to walk me to my car didn't seem so silly. Dave's bulging muscles were looking better every second.

As I buckled my seat belt, I squinted at the darker shadows at the other end of the parking lot. Was that a car parked over there?

I pulled out onto the highway and flipped open my phone. Talking to Carly would calm my nerves. I waited until the first curve was safely maneuvered then glanced down at my phone to hit Carly's speed-dial number. Headlights glared in my rearview mirror, and suddenly I felt a hard thump against my bumper. The vehicle behind me had come from nowhere. Had it bumped me? I slowed a little. If it had, it would surely back off now. *Bam!* The cell phone flew out of my hand, and I gripped the steering wheel tighter. The words of the anonymous letter flitted through my mind. Was the driver doing this on purpose? "Dear Lord," I murmured, "please, please help me."

I pushed the accelerator down, hoping to get away, but I felt a hard hit behind my door, and my car fishtailed. I had no idea whether to brake or speed up some more. Why hadn't I taken those defensive driving courses offered at the high school? I slammed on the brakes then screamed as my car hit the loose gravel on the shoulder of the road and the steering wheel spun out of my hands. "God, help me!"

I tried to hang on, but my body jerked against the seat belt as I bounced over terrain that was clearly not the road. When the swerving headlight beams showed a line of trees in front of me, I squeezed my eyes shut and braced for the impact.

I woke slowly, details of the strange room filtering into my sleep-fuddled brain. A television was suspended from the ceiling in the corner. My gaze slid sideways to rest on my dad, reading the *Monitor* and wearing a frown. My dad hardly ever frowned.

"Daddy?" I tried to say, but it was more like a croak.

He lowered the paper and jumped up. A smile spread across his face. "Jenna! How you doin'?"

"Hospital?"

He took my hand in his and caressed it with his thumb. "You had a little car accident."

"What happened?" Shadowy images flitted in and out of my semiconscious. Bright headlights. Then a hard bump from behind.

"We think maybe a deer ran out in front of you. Do you remember?"

I hesitated and felt my eyes close again. Sleep called me like a pied piper's song. "Sort of," I mumbled. "A car. Behind me. No deer."

"Okay, we can talk about it later, honey. You go ahead and rest."

The next time I woke, Daddy was gone, but Mama was there in the same chair, her gaze locked on my face, her brows knitted together with obvious worry. She smiled. "Hey, how's my baby?" She was using that hospital voice—almost a whisper but not quite.

"I'm okay."

"No, I mean how are you *really*?" She reached for my hand and squeezed. "You can tell me."

"I ache all over. My head hurts, and every time I breathe it feels as though someone is stabbing me." Well, that sounded whiney enough. I felt like crying.

"Oh, honey, I'm so sorry. You've got a lot of bruises and abrasions, but no concussion, at least. I'll call the nurse to give you some pain medicine."

"What I'd love is a Caramel Macchiato. Remember when Hayley had her tonsils out, we got one at the little coffee shop downstairs?" If she would go get me one, that would give me time to decide what to do about the memories that were rushing in like a river now that I was completely awake.

Mama's eyes lost some of their sadness and regained a little of their normal twinkle. "Good to see you're still yourself. And I'd be glad to go get you one, but I hate to leave you alone." She hesitated. "Do you remember much of last night?"

Leave it to Mama to get to the heart of the matter.

I nodded then immediately regretted it. My skull felt as though a little man with a big hammer had taken up residence inside. "Some. How did they find me?" Had the driver of the car behind me developed a conscience and called it in? Or was it a murderer with no conscience? I shuddered. I had to tell someone about being run off the road. But Mama, face already drawn with worry, wasn't my first choice.

"You called Carly. When she answered, she heard thumping noises and you praying aloud, then a scream. She called 911, and they headed out of town toward the health club, looking in all the ravines along the way with their spotlight. You'd gone down under a hill, but they found you within ten minutes, thankfully."

I closed my eyes. If I hadn't punched Carly's speed-dial button, I might still be in my car instead of safe in the hospital. "What about my car?" I loved that car.

"Sorry, baby, it's completely totaled. At least it's insured."

I closed my eyes against the tears that threatened to overflow.

"You can use my car until you get another one,"

Mama murmured. Her cool hand brushed across my head and a bandage I hadn't realized was there. "Go on back to sleep. You're going to be fine."

"I'm not sleepy. Just resting my eyes." *And thinking.* I stared at her and noticed something else behind the worry. Strength. Mama could handle the truth. "When I left the health club last night, I was calling Carly when I got to the second curve, and headlights came up behind me, fast. Then I felt a hard hit on my back bumper. Before I could react, the car pulled up beside me and rammed me."

She put her hand over her mouth but nodded. "That's about what we figured after what you said to your daddy earlier. He's gone to talk to John right now."

John? Great. Exactly what this day needed.

"Jenna, did you see who it was?"

"No, but there's more." I told her about the threatening letter.

She sank to the chair, her face almost as white as the wall behind her. "Honey, what have you gotten yourself into?"

"I'm doing it for Zac, Mama. And for Marge."

"Your dad and I would do anything to keep Zac from being arrested. But not risk your life. You've got to stop this snooping."

"I want to know." I stared at her eyes, so much like mine. How could she not understand? "I *need* to know."

She gave a half laugh. "You always have *needed*

to know. Needed to know what would happen if you mixed vinegar with baking soda, needed to know where that butterfly had gone or where the falling leaf would land. When you were little, you kept me busy rescuing you from your need to know." The smile faded. "But it's time to outgrow that insatiable curiosity. It's too dangerous."

Tears burned my eyelids. "I'm sorry, Mama."

She reached up and touched my cheek with her palm, tenderness evident in her eyes. "Promise me you'll be more careful."

"I promise." That was easy. I didn't want to end up in the hospital again. . .or worse. Besides, I had a date tonight. I intended to live long enough to find out if Alex Campbell was as special as I remembered. Although we might have to rethink that long walk beside the river. "Now how about some coffee?"

"I don't know about leaving you."

"No one is going to bother me in broad daylight with all these nurses and doctors running around."

She shoved the CALL button at me. "You keep this close and push it if a stranger comes in."

"I will." Anything to get my caffeine. No need to add that if the murderer was the one who ran me off the road; I seriously doubted the person would be a stranger.

After she left, I closed my eyes again and thanked God for getting me out of last night alive. The door creaked open slowly. My heartbeat accelerated, but I kept my eyes closed.

"Jenna? Jenna, are you asleep?" Brendan Stiles's quiet voice sounded close to my face. I resisted the urge to open my eyes and kept my finger resting lightly on the CALL button. If I screamed and pushed it at the same time. . .

Before the scream materialized, Brendan whispered, "I hope you can hear me. I need to tell you, you were right about Zac. He didn't kill Hank. But I think I know who did."

With no direction from my brain, my eyes flew open. Just like in the hall at the newspaper office that night, I was staring straight into Brendan's eyes. "Who?"

"Well, well!" A woman's voice echoed through the room. Brendan jerked upright, and I looked past him at Amelia, who had pulled her usual trick of entering a room with absolutely no noise. *Wonder if she'd teach me how to do that.* "I hope I'm not interrupting a tête-à-tête. I'd heard rumors that you two had a falling out. That should be a lesson to all of us not to listen to rumors."

I used the arrows to raise myself up to a semi-sitting position in the bed. "So, Amelia, what are you doing here?" That didn't sound right. Tact has never been my strong suit, but surely after the last twenty-four hours, I couldn't be expected to say everything perfectly. "I mean, how did you know I was here?" Well, that may have actually been worse given the circumstances. . .and the suspicions racing through my mind as I stared at my two surprise visitors. How *had* they known I was here? And had one of them tried to run me off the road?

Brendan began making those see-you-later noises, and I clutched his arm. I may not have been thinking clearly, but there was safety in numbers, and I was better off with both of them than one of them. "Stay here until Mama comes back. I'm sure she would love to see you."

"Well, I—" He looked at Amelia and paused.

I what? I can't kill you with her here? I'm still mad at you, so I don't mind if she bumps you off?

The door opened again before he could finish, and I let go of his arm. Marge bustled into the room, Lois in her wake, each with a vase of flowers. My hospital room was obviously the place to be in Lake View this morning. The recurring question was, how did they all know I was here?

Marge froze when she saw Amelia. The two sisters stared at each other without a word. Emotions flickered across both of their faces so quickly I couldn't begin to name them all. Then Amelia looked at me. "Darling, I must go. Sorry for barging in on you lovebirds. When Byron's whispering in my ear, I surely don't want to be interrupted." She gave an airy wave and swept from the room.

Lois frowned and plunked her flowers down on the windowsill. "*Humph.* What was *she* doing here?"

"She just dropped by to. . ."—I actually had no idea—". . .see me. How are you ladies doing today?"

Marge seemed to snap out of the trance she'd been in ever since she saw Amelia. "We're doing okay, but what about you?" She set her floral arrangement beside Lois's, hurried to my side, and kissed my forehead.

"I'd better run, Jenna." Brendan had edged closer to the door without my realizing it.

"Okay." I gave him what I hoped was a private, meaningful glance. "We'll talk later."

He nodded, yanked the door open, and hurried out.

"How'd you know I was here?" I directed the question to either of the two women.

"Lois took me to breakfast at the diner for my birthday. Debbie told us a customer heard it on the scanner."

The scanner. Of course. Lake View's version of the town crier. Maybe I should get one.

"Happy birthday." My reply was instinctive. Sadly enough, Amelia had to have known it was her sister's birthday, yet she'd not said a word.

Marge nodded. "Did a deer run out in front of you and cause you to swerve off the road?" Concern laced her voice.

"That area out there sure is rife with deer this time of year," Lois offered before I could answer. "Last week, I had a huge buck dart out right in front of me." She shuddered. "Thought I was going to plow into it, but I was careful not to swerve."

"They taught us that in the defensive driving course we took over at the school last year," Marge said.

I knew I should have taken that course when they offered it this year.

"So is that what happened to you?" Marge asked again.

I had no idea what to say. Thankfully, Mama walked in right then with my Caramel Macchiato. Amid all the greetings, the question was apparently forgotten.

While they chatted, I closed my eyes and listened to the comfortable bedside chitchat. Sarah Hutchins had her baby. Little Joy Fields fell on the monkey bars at school and broke her arm. There was a time before Hank's murder when those things *were* the news in Lake View. Would we ever get back there again?

Someone was watching me. Intently. I peeked through my eyelashes at Alex's well-sculptured face.

"Hey, water girl, you okay?"

I opened my eyes completely. "I think so. They're supposed to let me go home this afternoon." If he'd come to the hospital to cancel our date, he could forget about it. I wasn't letting him off that easily.

"I know you probably don't feel like going out tonight. . . ."

I couldn't believe it. He was ditching me in a hospital room. "Is this why you ignored my messages? Because you didn't want to go out with me?" Might as well find out now.

"Technically, I didn't ignore your messages; I just didn't get them." A sheepish smile spread across his reddening face. "Here's the thing. I washed my cell phone."

"In the washer?"

He nodded. "I admit I'm not much at washing clothes or keeping house. But I do have my redeeming qualities."

"Like what?" *A heart-melting smile?*

"It's been said that I'm not a bad cook. So as I was saying. . ." He drew his brows together in mock sternness. "Since you're probably not up to going out tonight, I was wondering if you might want some company."

"That would be nice," I said, suddenly shy.

A smile spread across his face. "Do you mind if I come over a little early and make us some supper?"

Did I mind? What could be more decadent than reclining on the couch while a man cooked the meal? "Perfect."

"Okay, then, I'll see you about five." He leaned toward me and I held my breath. I kept my eyes open, though, in case he was just brushing a speck of lunch off my face. At least they'd taken the little heart-rate thingy off my finger. Otherwise I was sure the nurses would be rushing in to see why my pulse had gone off the chart.

In my limited experience, hugs over hospital bed-rails are not usually life-changing. But as I returned Alex's gentle embrace and breathed in the familiar scent of his soap, I felt so blessed with second chances. A second chance to live after last night. And after all these years, a second chance to love.

"I'm glad you're okay," he whispered in my ear, then released me.

I shivered.

"Are you cold?"

"No, um—" How embarrassing.

His smile crinkled the corners of his eyes. "Good." He leaned in and brushed his lips to mine. "See you tonight."

I waved good-bye as he walked out the door.

When Carly came in a few minutes later, I was still smiling.

Lake View Monitor

Fᴜɴ Qᴜɪᴢ ᴏꜰ ᴛʜᴇ Wᴇᴇᴋ

**Are You a Stiletto
or a Sneaker?**

1. Your idea of a great time
is to:

   (a) go to Chez La Troque
for a scrumptious five-course
meal and possible celebrity
sighting

   (b) get a burger and fries
from the local Dairy Bar on
your way to a rousing game of
putt-putt

2. The perfect guy for this
date is:

   (a) Vin Diesel
   (b) Orlando Bloom

Even another run-in with the chief of police couldn't
ruin my mood. At least John hadn't accused me of
forcing myself off the road. As a matter of fact, I'm
pretty sure that beneath his gruff questioning was concern for me. A concern my family shared. Carly took

me home with strict orders from our parents not to leave me until Alex got there. She was going to come back when he left. Although I don't know what they thought she'd do if someone came after me again.

I pushed END on my cell phone. "I still can't get Brendan to answer. I left him another message to call me."

Carly came out of my closet with a red T-shirt in her hand. "Here, try this one. If he knows who killed Hank, wonder why he doesn't go to John?"

"I don't know." I'd settled on jeans, but finding the perfect top was proving a challenge. It was hard to find something that coordinated perfectly with the bandage on my forehead.

As I tried on the shirt, Carly plopped down on the bed. "Does this remind you of when I used to get ready for dates with Travis? You'd watch me, ever ready to give your opinion."

"Yes, and even as a thirteen-year-old, I had no sense of style."

"You didn't need a sense of style. Still don't. Anything looks good on you."

"Yeah, right." I turned from the mirror to look at her. "Did I tell you I took a coffee quiz the other day online?"

"A coffee quiz?" Carly looked at me as if I'd lost my mind.

"Yeah, to tell you what kind of coffee you are." I smoothed down my red T-shirt over my jeans. "No big surprise I turned out to be a plain old cup of joe."

Carly nodded. "Well, you're in luck. Think about

it. Most men prefer a plain old cup of joe."

"Uh-oh." I met her eyes in the mirror.

"Uh-oh?" She pushed off the bed and walked over to stand beside me.

I grinned at her reflection. "I took it for you, too. You're a cappuccino."

"Then I'll have to find a special man, won't I?" She blushed and ran her hand through her short curls.

"Carly Elizabeth. What happened to my man-hater sister?"

"I never hated men." She picked up a denim vest from the pile of discarded outfits draped across my chair. "I couldn't trust them. I'm still not sure I can. Put this on."

"But my shirt isn't tucked in."

She rolled her eyes. "Just put it on."

I slipped into it and turned back to the mirror. The red T-shirt was three inches longer than the open vest. Even though I'd have never considered wearing it that way, it worked. "Perfect. Casual but different. How do you do that?"

The doorbell rang, and my gaze flew to the clock. "It's five already. He's right on time."

"You look beautiful."

We started down the hallway, and I stopped. "I can't believe I'm this nervous. This is Alex, the boy who gave me a frog for my eighth birthday. What am I worried about?"

Carly studied my face. "That you might go out there and find a stranger in his place?"

"That's it. What if it's all been a schoolgirl fantasy, and we don't click anymore?"

"Then it's better to know and be done with it. I'm going to slip out the back door while you answer the front."

"Sure you don't want to stay?"

She laughed. "I'm positive. Call me when he leaves and I'll be over to stay the night, though. I'm looking forward to our sleepover. Even if I am just playing the role of bodyguard."

We hugged carefully, being mindful of my bruised shoulder, and then she was gone.

I opened the front door to find Alex, his arms laden with grocery bags. "Let me help you with that."

"Thanks, but I've got it. Just show me the kitchen."

I led the way into my small kitchen. "Can I help?"

He unloaded his arms and motioned toward a bar stool. "If you'd hold that stool down, I'd appreciate it." He grinned. "Seriously, I'd love it if you want to talk while I cook. You need to be resting."

"I've been resting all day," I said, but I sat down anyway. It's amazing how a little car crash can sap your energy.

"Do you know what happened last night?"

"Did you eat lunch at the diner?"

He nodded.

"Then you probably know as much as I do."

"Is it true someone ran you off the road?"

" 'Fraid so."

He frowned. "Can you leave this alone?"

I shook my head.

"I was afraid of that."

I sighed. How many times could one person get the same lecture? I was going for the Olympic record. "Do you mind if we don't talk about this tonight? I've already promised Mama I'd be more careful. For now, I want to forget it."

"Sure."

For the next few minutes, Alex got acquainted with my kitchen and kept up a running commentary about the food he was preparing. He opened a bag of salad into a bowl and sprinkled shredded cheese, real bacon bits, and chopped tomatoes on top of it. "Ranch?" he asked.

"Do you have to ask?" We'd both always loved Ranch dressing.

"I was hoping you still felt that way. It's the only kind I brought."

When the oven was preheated, he popped the rolls in and placed the salmon on the indoor grill. "Hope you don't mind that we're keeping it simple tonight."

"This is simple?" I tried to raise an eyebrow but failed miserably. I might as well face it. At almost thirty, chances weren't good that I would suddenly be able to pull off that little feat. Especially with the bandage on my head. "For me, this is gourmet. When did you start cooking?"

"Right after college. I dated a girl who loved to cook, and I was fascinated by all the dishes she made. It didn't take long for me to realize I could save myself a lot of headache and learn to cook."

As soon as he said the words "dated a girl," jealousy seared through my stomach. It wasn't like I thought he hadn't dated, but he'd said it so casually.

"So you left her brokenhearted?" My smile felt forced. Was this his normal way of doing business? Love 'em and leave 'em? Maybe I'd just been the first in a long string of women who started using his brand of soap after he left so they could still feel close to him.

He froze with the seasoning shaker suspended above the salmon. "Not hardly." He narrowed his eyes. "Is that what you think of me?"

"I don't know what to think of you," I said quietly, my stomach churning. Why hadn't I saved this conversation until after supper?

"Let's make a deal," he said as he seasoned the salmon.

"What?"

He plunked the shaker down on the table. "We'll enjoy the meal and each other's company. Then afterwards, we'll sit down and talk." He extended his hand. "Deal?"

I hesitated. Could I do it? My heart desperately wanted this time with him. I put my own hand in his. "Deal."

While we ate, we reminisced, but by unspoken agreement, we limited our nostalgic journey to the years before we dated. As we finished up, he set his glass on the table. "How's Carly doing now, really? I can't believe she never remarried."

"She handles it pretty well, I think, but she has some trust issues." I thought of her sauna confession about Elliott, but I wasn't about to tell Alex about that.

"Remember how you cried when she ran off with Travis to get married?" he asked.

I nodded. "Almost like I knew what would happen, but in reality I was just fourteen and it felt like I lost my big sister. I couldn't believe she kept it a secret from me. She was afraid I'd feel like I should tell Mom and Dad."

"Which you probably would have."

"True. But I still felt betrayed. That's why I ran off to the tree house."

"I could hear your sobs before I even got up the ladder. But I'd have known where you were even if I hadn't." His voice was soft with memories.

"That day. . ." He'd held me while I cried. When I stopped, I must have been a sight, but he wiped the tears from my cheeks and looked at me as if I was beautiful. My best friend was suddenly much more.

He touched my hand. "Our first kiss."

So much for boundaries. I slipped my hand out from under his. "So now that supper's over, the deal is off?"

He sat back and blew out his breath. "I guess so. Where do we even begin?"

I stood and picked up my plate. He took it from me. "Why don't you let me clean up?"

"Don't you think you've done enough?" Oh, that

was a classic Jenna-ism. "I didn't mean—"

He chuckled. "I know what you meant."

"We can just leave this. I'll clean it up later," I said.

"Let's deal with it tonight. It'll just be harder to face tomorrow."

I nodded. Why did everything have to have a double meaning? We'd been so relaxed earlier, but now tension crackled in the air. We worked in silence for a while, and when the dishwasher was running, he touched my arm. "I forgot to tell you—you look nice tonight."

"Thanks." Heat crept up my face. "So do you."

He laughed. "You don't have to say that."

"No, it's true. . . ." My voice faded off. Was I actually standing in my kitchen telling Alex Campbell I liked how he looked? "Let's go sit down for a minute—and relax," I added under my breath.

"Sounds good."

I led the way to the living room, where Carly had left an eighties CD repeating softly when we first got home from the hospital. Had she planned this? And figured I needed all the help I could get? Probably.

"Oh, man. It's been a long time since I heard that song." Alex sank onto the couch and patted the spot beside him.

I sat—not quite at the opposite end of the sofa but not right next to him, either. Distance made my mind work better, and I wanted to think as clearly as possible while we had the discussion I'd been dreading since I first heard Alex was back in town.

He laughed. "I don't remember your being this prickly."

I tossed him a quick, totally insincere smile. "Maybe I didn't have a reason to be prickly then."

"You?" He pushed back against the sofa back and crossed his feet in front of him. "Deep down, I knew our relationship always came second to your swimming. But I never realized you'd break up with me because you lost a swim meet."

"A swim meet?" I jumped to my feet, then put my hand on my bandage. Whoa. No more sudden movements. He saw me and in a second was on his feet beside me, but I pushed him away. "It was the Olympics! Besides, I didn't break up with you!"

I walked over to the window and stared blindly out at the sunset. If I faced him, he'd see the tears sparkling in my eyes, and I wasn't ready to completely trash my pride.

"What do you call refusing to talk to me?" His voice sounded close behind me.

I steadied myself against the windowsill and kept my eyes fixed on the fading day. "I call it needing some time to come to grips with the fact that I let the whole nation down."

"What about letting me down?"

I turned around, amazed by his bluntness. He was less than a foot away. "You were included in the whole nation. And yes, you most of all. You believed in me. So did your dad. And I flubbed up."

"Dad said you had a bad cold."

I rolled my eyes. "Don't even try to make excuses for me. I wasn't good enough. I lost."

"Okay."

"Okay." I was obstinately pained that he gave in so quickly, but at least we knew where we stood now.

"So what if you weren't good enough? Did that give you the right to throw away our future?"

I'd thrown away our future? Had I stumbled into one of the endless strings of kids' movies where the main characters swap bodies? "I'm not the one who left."

"You knew I was going to college. I sent flowers, I called you, I even came over, but your mama said you weren't up to seeing anyone. I tried everything."

Suddenly I remembered the flowers. White daisies and red roses. I'd felt so unworthy that I'd thrown them out. Was Alex right? Had I overreacted? Was I partly to blame? I pressed my back against the windowsill, letting it support my weight. The thought made me dizzy. "Thank you for the flowers. They were beautiful."

His eyes widened, and he gave an incredulous laugh. "Why didn't you say that then?"

"I was ashamed."

He shook his head. "Until the other day when we were eating at the diner, I thought you blamed me because my dad and mom moved away and left you."

My turn to laugh. "We messed things up good, didn't we? I was so self-centered to think that the world revolved around the Olympics."

"I should have tried harder to get through to you. I let my pride get in the way."

"Is that why you never tried again to contact me once you went away to college?" I had to know. Deep down even then I'd realized the way I acted after the Olympics was wrong. But I never expected him to just forget about me.

"I didn't want to be rejected again. By the time I got over that, it seemed that it had been too long."

"I'm sorry." I didn't mind saying it first. Pride wasn't all it was cracked up to be.

"Me, too." He reached for me, and I didn't pull away. "I wish I'd tried harder."

He traced my lips with his thumb and kissed me on the cheek. "Do-over?"

"Yes," I whispered as he brought his lips to mine. The ghosts of the past had been laid to rest. There was no strong sense of the familiar, no reawakening of a childhood romance. There was just me—almost thirty but far from desperate—kissing a strong Christian man I could easily imagine spending the rest of my life with.

"Lucky you moved back to Lake View, or we'd have never known, I guess," I said a few minutes later.

He grinned and raised one eyebrow. "Luck had nothing to do with it."

A buzzing noise jarred me awake. I lay still in the dark for a minute, listening to Carly breathe. I'd been deeply engrossed in a vivid dream. Alex and I were on jet skis, racing each other across the lake. We were both laughing, when suddenly a big wall emerged from the water, and he went to the left of it and I went to the right. No matter how far I went, there was never a break in the wall or a place to cut over to him. Some dreams weren't worth analyzing.

I fumbled around on the nightstand and winked at the red numbers on my alarm clock—5:29 a.m.

Beside the clock, my cell phone was lit up. I picked it up and looked at the screen. ONE NEW MESSAGE. I held it in my hand as I relaxed back on my pillow. "Dumb phone." Sometimes it wouldn't show I had a new message until hours after the fact. Unfortunately, I never thought to check them until it buzzed.

"Um, Jenna. . ." Carly's sleep-blurred voice sounded beside me.

"Yeah?"

"You might be going a little overboard with the animal thing."

I raised myself up on one elbow and looked over at her. A shadowy figure I recognized as Mr. Persi was sprawled out on top of her, and Neuro was curled up on her feet. I laughed. "You wanted me to commit."

"Yeah, but I had something a little more human in mind," she mumbled.

"Well, don't start planning the wedding, but at least I'm working on that." I shooed the animals off the bed and sat up. Mr. Persi usually came and got in my bed when he needed to go out.

She kept her eyes closed, but she smiled. We'd talked until one thirty or so about my date.

"What about you?"

Her eyes opened. "What about me what?"

"Have you seen Elliott lately?"

She gave a negative grunt and turned her back to

me. "I need sleep."

I pressed the phone against my ear as I stumbled down the hall, the dog at my heels. The automated voice said, "You have one message sent at 9:34 p.m." Of course, I'd left the phone upstairs while I was with Alex.

I opened the back door and listened to the message as Mr. Persi bounded into the backyard. "Jenna? It's Brendan. I still need to talk to you. It's urgent. Call me in the morning or just come by. I'll be up by six." Silence crackled on the line, then, "And, Jenna, please don't tell anyone I called."

I saved the message. A dreadful howl sounded from the porch, and I hurriedly opened the door. Mr. Persi shot in. Not long after I had allowed him into my house to stay, I solved the mystery of that first night's episode of horrible howling on the porch. The dog was highly attuned to sirens. Even when I couldn't hear them, he could. And they apparently inspired him to mock them. "You ambulance chaser, you," I grumbled as he padded down the hall to go back to bed.

Twenty minutes later, I'd showered and dressed. Carly, still dead to the world in Animal Kingdom, burrowed deeper into her pillow. I knew she'd be mad at me for not waking her, but if I let her go with me, Brendan might clam up. Not a chance I could afford to take. I scrawled a quick message explaining my departure and ended with—

If you don't hear from me by seven, come after me. And bring the cavalry.

Love, Jenna

I quietly set the alarm clock for 7:00 a.m. and put the note on my pillow.

In the garage, reality hit me. My wonderful old Volvo, my faithful friend since I bought it my first year of teaching, was now a totaled heap in a junkyard somewhere. I glanced at Carly's van. She wouldn't mind my borrowing it, once she got over being mad at me for going without her. But then she'd be stuck without a ride if she needed to come get me. The bicycle on the wall rack caught my eye. My body, still bruised from the car accident, flinched at the idea. *C'mon, Jenna, you can do it.* Brendan's house was less than two miles, especially if I cut through the park.

Visions of Hank lying motionless behind a bush flashed through my mind. On second thought, maybe going through the park before daylight was a bad idea. It wouldn't save me over five minutes.

I stretched my sore muscles for a minute then climbed gingerly onto the bike and pedaled down the dark road. The streetlamps lent an eerie glow to the neighborhood street. Not a soul in sight.

When I turned onto Liberty Road, I paused with my feet still on the pedals for a second. If Brendan turned out to be the murderer, I'd have no neighbor to yell for. Instead of next door to each other, houses were half a mile apart out here. Some, like the mayor's, were mansions, while others, like the up-and-coming pharmacist's, were more modest. I put all my energy into pedaling. An early riser had been burning leaves or something, and the acrid smell of smoke wafted to me.

Carly would wake up in less than an hour and come right over with the cavalry if I didn't call her first. If Brendan was the killer, which I'd stake my life he wasn't. . . Wait—I actually was staking my life that he wasn't. But if he was, I'd have to stall him until help came. And pray.

Almost there. I pumped hard to get up the last big hill. When I crested it, I tapped my brakes instinctively and gaped at Brendan's house. Or what was left of it, which wasn't much. Two fire trucks on each side of the driveway flanked John's police car. My mind spun as fast as my tires as I coasted down the hill and into the driveway.

John had his back to me, talking to a fireman, but the man motioned to me and John spun around. "Jenna! What are you doing here?" His florid face was streaked with black, and his eyes looked as though he'd been up all night.

I braked to a skidding stop. "Brendan asked me to come. I needed to talk to him." I stared over his shoulder at the tiny tendrils of smoke curling up from the ashy remains of the house. "Where is he?"

His tired eyes filled with compassion as he put his hand on my shoulder. Oh no. Had the killer gotten to Brendan before I could?

"I'm sorry," John murmured. "He's dead."

My legs buckled. John lowered me to a sitting position on the cold driveway and squatted down beside me.

Hot tears splashed down my cheeks.

"I didn't know you were that close."

I shook my head. "He knew who the murderer was," I croaked, the smell of smoke suddenly choking me. "He wanted to tell me."

"No, Jenna, honey. . ." John smoothed my hair down with his beefy hand as I sobbed against his jacket. "He *was* the murderer. And he wanted to kill you."

Lake View Monitor

LOCAL MAN DIES IN FIRE

A mysterious fire has apparently claimed the life of Lake View pharmacist Brendan Stiles. Firefighters were called to the residence at 1422 Liberty Road at 3:00 a.m. Saturday morning by an anonymous 911 call. By the time they arrived, the entire house was in flames. No further details are available at this time.

The sky lightened gradually as I sat with my back against a tree, praying about Brendan, praying for Marge, praying for practically the whole town, while I watched the crime-scene crew gingerly pick through the coolest part of the ruins. John had gone to greet them and give them instructions, leaving me denying his accusations of Brendan.

"I'll prove it to you in a minute. Stay put!" he'd ordered.

"Jenna! Are you okay?" Carly collapsed beside me,

her brightly colored Tweety Bird pajamas morbidly incongruous with the scene, her face blotchy and red. Tears streaked down her cheeks.

"Oh, Carly!" I fell against her. "I'm so sorry." I motioned toward the ruins. "I forgot to call you."

"I tried to bring the cavalry, but the desk sergeant said they were already here. Betty felt sorry for me and told me what happened."

"You're in your pajamas." She surely knew it, but I just couldn't grasp the fact that she'd rushed out without getting dressed. I was the sister who did that kind of thing.

"Surely you didn't think I'd take time to dress when the alarm went off at seven and you weren't there."

"I'm sorry," I groaned. "Did Betty tell you that Brendan's dead?"

"Yes." She lowered her voice. "And that he's the murderer. She could probably get fired for that, but like I said, I guess she felt sorry for me."

"That part we'll talk about later. John's got some harebrained idea that Brendan meant to kill me this morning, but if that's the case, why did he kill himself and burn his house down?"

She shrugged. "Who knows?"

"Who all did you call while you were driving over here?" I waved weakly at Daddy, who was walking toward us.

"Everyone on speed dial."

A familiar truck squealed to a stop in the driveway

just as Daddy got to us. "Is Alex on your speed dial?"

She twisted around and watched as he jumped out of the truck. " 'Fraid so."

Daddy hugged us both quickly. "You all right?"

We nodded.

"Let me find out what's going on, girls," he said and strode across the lawn to where John stood.

"That's Daddy. Take-Charge Stafford. Get answers and get 'em now," I said quietly.

"Humph." Carly looked from him to me. "Looks like someone's a chip off the old block."

"You make a habit of slipping out before daylight to go meet murderers?"

I spun around.

Alex's face was a study of puzzlement and pain.

"Only when they invite me."

He pulled me close. "You scared me to death."

"I'm sorry. It made perfect sense at the time." I relaxed for a minute against him then pushed back and looked at him. "Besides, I don't think he's the murderer."

"Then maybe you need to take a look at this." John's gruff voice cut into our conversation. He held out a note sealed in a ziplock bag. "We found this taped to the mailbox," he said grimly.

Alex took it and read aloud, " 'I'm sorry about Hank. It wasn't supposed to happen that way. And tell Jenna I'm sorry for what I almost did to her.' " He looked up at me bleakly. "It's signed 'Brendan Stiles.' "

John looked at the four of us. "This information

isn't to leave this circle. Are we clear on that?"

We all nodded.

"The way we figure it, Hank got wind that Brendan was dealing drugs illegally. Hank's autopsy results came in a week or so ago. Turns out a drug overdose was the real cause of his death. The golf club was just an added bonus."

"So naturally that means the pharmacist did it."

John glared at me and waved the plastic bag at me. "When you have a signed confession, it does."

"Well, that's certainly convenient, isn't it?" I asked, and they all turned as one to look at me. "Brendan's dead. And he's the murderer. Oh, and he ran me off the road."

John nodded. "That about sums it up, the best we can figure it."

"Well, maybe you need to start refiguring. Mama always told me that when something looked too good to be true, it probably was." I picked up my bike and sat it up on its wheels. "Murderers don't normally tie themselves up in a neat little bow." I rolled the bicycle over to Alex's truck, leaving them to think whatever they wanted.

"You want a hand with that?" Alex asked.

I scrutinized his face. "You on my side? Or you think I'm crazy?"

"I tend to agree with you, but I think maybe you should use a bit more discretion. Try a little harder not to get yourself killed." He took the bike and put his hand over mine with the same motion. "There are people who'd be extremely disappointed if that happened."

"Like you?" I asked, and relinquished the bike as he lifted it effortlessly into the bed of the truck.

His eyes flickered back to where Daddy and Carly were locked in deep conversation, no doubt debating my sanity. "Among others. But yes, definitely me."

I could see the concern in his eyes. Underneath the banter, Alex needed me to reassure him. He was worried about me. That should have annoyed me, but it didn't.

"I promise, Alex, from now on discretion is my middle name."

"Good." He pulled me gently into his arms. I inhaled his clean soap smell, almost forgetting the horrific scene behind me and the danger that might lie ahead.

Wednesday afternoon, I waited until I knew Amelia was in the pool, then turned to Gail. "I'm going to lunch. See you in an hour."

In the locker room, I slipped into a swimsuit and picked up a towel. At least three times a week, I swam in the mornings before we opened, but usually I avoided the pool during normal business hours. Too many people gawking to see if I ever had a chance at the Olympic gold.

I breathed a prayer of thanks when I entered the pool area. Other than Amelia swimming laps and a young mother with two little girls splashing in the far corner kiddie pool, the place was deserted.

I dove in on the opposite side from Amelia and swam a little underwater. *Discreet. Discreet.* I said the word over and over in my mind with each stroke. *Lord, please give me a natural opening.*

I surfaced and glanced around. No Amelia. Had she slipped out while I was swimming?

"Looks like someone's feeling better."

I turned and she was perched on the side of the pool, her lemon-yellow bikini showing off her trim figure.

I wiped the water from my face with one hand. "Amelia. Hi." Not brilliant. But discreet.

"Hi." Her makeup was apparently waterproof and quite possibly bulletproof. Other than her slicked-back hair, she looked like she was ready to go out. "Glad you made it out of the hospital."

"Yeah, me, too."

"I'm sorry about Brendan." She actually looked uncomfortable. "I hope that wasn't too painful for you."

"Actually, in spite of what you thought at the hospital, we weren't involved."

She nodded. "Oh. Good. I found it hard to believe you were. Even before we found out he killed Hank, he didn't seem your type."

A shriek from the kiddie pool drew our attention. The two little girls in their ruffled two-piece bathing suits were pulling on a blow-up doughnut. "Mine! Mine!" they screamed in chorus.

Amelia rolled her eyes. "Some people need to learn to control their children."

"Well, you know sisters. . . ," I said. "They don't always treat each other the best." The old me would have said something about not mentioning birthdays, but the new discreet me just left it at that.

"You wouldn't let anyone come between you and your sister, would you?"

I shook my head. "Not if I could help it." Who did she mean specifically? Hank? Or Byron? Or both?

To my amazement, a genuine smile broke across Amelia's face. "You're a scrapper, aren't you?"

I didn't know how to answer. Was I? And if I was, should I admit it?

"I like that about you, Jenna. A lot of people think you've settled, giving up on the Olympics, then quitting teaching. Moving back home to work here." She waved a well-manicured hand at the pool area. "But I have a feeling about you. You're just preparing. Regrouping. When the time comes for you to decide your future, you'll know what to do."

I nodded. Had Obi-Wan Kenobi disguised himself as Amelia Stanton? Her words sounded like a fortune-cookie message, but oddly enough, I was touched. "Thanks, Amelia."

"Don't thank me. I know all about regrouping."

Discreet. "Really?"

"Yes." She slipped off the rim of the pool and into the water, then swam to the other side. I had little choice but to go back to swimming myself. Apparently along with discretion came baby steps and patience.

I was alone in the locker room, tying my shoelaces, when she came in. Faced with now or never, I kicked my newfound diplomacy out the door. "I understand you and Byron have an alibi for Hank's murder."

Her laughter trilled through the air, and she pointed at me. "I was right about you. I knew I was." She whirled the combination lock on her locker. "What difference does it make? Everybody knows Brendan Stiles was the killer. Even though he wasn't your boyfriend, that was still a shock, wasn't it?"

"Mm-hmm."

She looked at me. "You don't think he did it?"

I shrugged. "I don't know."

"Byron and I have already given our alibis to John."

"Oh?"

Her smile faded, and her eyebrows knitted together. "Leave it alone, Jenna."

"I'm a scrapper, remember?"

"That's good. To an extent. But you need to learn

to mind your own business, before you get hurt. . .or worse." She snatched up her clothes and her towel and sashayed toward the shower without another word.

I sat on the bench for a minute longer thinking about what she'd said. Those words sounded strangely familiar. What big secret were the mayor of Lake View and his charming first lady hiding? And more importantly, had Amelia just threatened to kill me?

During my Friday inspection of the weight room equipment, my cell phone vibrated. A text message from Alex appeared on the screen. WANT TO GO CAR SHOPPING THIS AFTERNOON? A smile tilted my lips. Those words might not seem romantic to most people, but only someone who cared about me would realize how tired I was of driving Mama's Buick and how much I needed my own wheels.

SURE, I typed back. PICK ME UP AT 4:30 AT HOME, OKAY?

SEE YOU THEN.

With a lighter spirit, I went back to my inspection.

Bob stuck his head in. "Jenna, can we talk in the office for a few minutes?"

I'd been trying to have a private conversation with him ever since he got back from his cruise, but he'd avoided me like I was a persistent telemarketer. Now *he* wanted to talk to *me*?

In the office, he took one of the two chairs beside our desks and motioned me to the other. A good sign? If he'd wanted to make me feel inferior, he'd have surely sat in his own big leather chair and put me across from him in the job-applicant chair. Maybe he was finally ready to treat me as an equal and sell me the business.

"The thing is. . ." He cleared his throat. "You know I've talked about selling the business."

Yes, you've talked about selling the business to me. *How could I not know?* I wanted to scream. But Mama always said you caught more flies with honey than vinegar. So I just said, "Yes, sir?"

He studied the chair arm and picked a loose thread from between his fingers. "I still want to sell it."

Okay, good. And?

"Remember my daughter, Lisa?"

I nodded. She'd been behind me in school, but while we were in college, she'd married a very wealthy older man. I hardly ever saw her, but I'd been by their house a few times, a big mansion with black wrought-iron gates, not too far from town. According to Bob, she did all of her business in Little Rock or Memphis. I'd often wondered why they even settled here, but that wasn't something you could just ask.

"She's. . ."—he cleared his throat again and picked harder at the thread—". . .having some trouble."

"Trouble? Is it her health?" He looked positively gray.

"Marriage trouble," he whispered. "She's moved back home with Wilma and me."

"Oh. I'm sorry."

"Me, too." Bob shook his head. "The thing is. . .she wants to work here."

"Work here?" What little I remembered of Lisa made Amelia look like Ellie Mae Clampett.

He nodded. "She needs something to do. A chance to get out of the house for a while. I was hoping you might train her to do your job, take her under your wing. Just until she gets her bearings."

"My job?" I'd become a parrot, but this conversation couldn't have been further from what I'd expected.

He looked at my face, no doubt seeing the shock there. "Oh, she won't be taking your job. I just want her to know a little more about the family business."

"The family business?" Polly want a cracker? I could surely do better than that. "Correct me if I'm wrong, Bob, but didn't you promise to sell me this business?"

"Sure did, sure did. And I still will if you'll just hang with me. But in the meantime, this will keep Lisa busy. Give her a chance to feel good about herself." He winked at me. Actually winked at me. "When she's back on her feet, then we'll get your name on the deed to this place." He stood.

I jumped up. "Bob, I—"

I don't know what I was going to say. Probably something closer to vinegar than to honey. But before I could speak, he said, "I know you're in a hurry to buy this place. And I aim to see that happen. But just to show you that I mean what I say, I'm giving you a raise effective Monday."

"A raise?" If he thought that raising my barely-above-poverty wage fifty cents more would make everything okay, he'd totally lost it.

He named a figure.

"Could you repeat that?"

He did, and I sat back down. The bottom line—he'd just raised my income level to that of my former teaching salary. I remembered what I told John the day of Brendan's fire—"*If something looks too good to be true. . .*" "Why would you do this?"

"You keep things going around here. And I use your name for advertising. That brings in a lot of business." He cleared his throat again and avoided my eyes. "Plus, I know you'll be real good to Lisa, and I want you to know in advance how much I appreciate that."

Oh brother. She must be even worse than I remembered if he was willing to cut into his profits to bribe me to be nice to her. But what could I say? I needed a new car.

I'd just climbed into Alex's truck when my cell phone rang. I glanced at the caller ID and shot Alex an apologetic glance. "Sorry, I'd better get this. I don't know who it is, but it's a local number. Hello?"

"Jenna?" An unfamiliar female voice came over the line.

"Yes?"

"This is Debbie. Over at the diner?"

"Oh, hi, Debbie." I immediately felt guilty that I was with Alex. When she'd asked me about him at the diner, I *hadn't* been dating him. "What's up?"

"Remember how you asked me to call if I heard anything or remembered anything about Hank?" Her voice was low.

"Yes?"

"I know everybody's saying Brendan is the murderer, but are you still interested in information?" she whispered.

"Definitely. Tell me." I strained to listen.

"Today at lunch, I was carrying food to the Stantons' table. The mayor and his wife had their heads together, and before they knew I was there, I heard her say, 'Thought it would be over after Hank was out of the picture.' Then she said something so low I couldn't hear, but she finished with, 'Jenna Stafford nosing around.' "

I heard muffled voices in the background; then Debbie hollered, "Be right there!" And in a quieter tone to me, "I've got to go."

"Thanks," I said to a dead line.

As Alex and I drove into town, I told him word for word what Debbie had said.

"You think they did it?"

"A Bonnie and Clyde type deal?" I mused. "I don't know. They strike me more like Barbie and Ken."

He snorted. "Barbie and Ken? The dolls?"

"Yep." I thought of Amelia yesterday, sitting on the poolside, her makeup perfect. "Sort of plastic. But not necessarily all bad."

"Oh, something I've been meaning to tell you. . ."

"Yeah?" His voice sounded so serious that I dreaded hearing his words.

He waited until we rolled to a stop at the red light, then turned to look at me. "I didn't say this the other day. But I'm sorry about Brendan. Since you dated him, I mean."

"Thanks. We weren't very close, but I appreciate it." I traced the *J* on my purse with my finger. "But I'm afraid he was killed because he was about to tell me who murdered Hank. I hate feeling like I'm somehow responsible."

He reached across the seat and took my hand in his. "Is that why you quit teaching?"

My gaze slid to his face. "You heard about that, huh?"

"Yeah, but I'd rather hear it from you." He caressed my skin with his thumb. "If you want to tell me about it." The light changed, and he let go of my hand. I felt the loss.

"One of my students had an undiagnosed heart

valve problem. We were doing some simple calisthenics. Nothing strenuous. But his heart stopped." I pushed my hair back from my face and looked up at the truck ceiling, trying not to see fifteen-year-old Colton lying lifeless on the gym floor. "I did CPR until the paramedics arrived." Memories of never-ending compressions and breaths flooded over me. "He didn't make it."

Alex pulled into the first car lot and parked. "Jenna, I'm sorry that happened. But you weren't responsible."

"I know. At first. . .maybe I thought that. I was mixed up, mad at God, madder at myself. But I found a good Christian counselor, and that helped a lot. Logically, I know his death wasn't my fault."

He got out of the truck and ran around to get my door. When I was on my feet, he hugged me. "I'm proud of you for getting past that. I can't believe how strong you are."

I laughed. "Just wait until you get to know me better."

"I can't wait." He dropped a quick kiss on my mouth. "But for now, let's get you some wheels."

Unfortunately, that was harder than it sounded. After perusing several different car lots, we were both exhausted by the time we got to Honest Larry's Car Sales. "You sure you want to stop here?" Alex asked as we pulled in.

"Because of the name?" I shrugged. "Dad says he is an honest car dealer." I gave him a rueful grin. "Besides, we've looked everywhere else in town."

He raised an eyebrow. "And the fact that you're

practically drooling over that silver Mustang out front has nothing to do with it, right?"

"Hey, cut a girl some slack, okay?"

He shook his head. "Gotta keep you on your toes."

Amazing how easily we'd gotten back into our old banter. He kept me on my toes all right. Every time I thought of him, my feet barely touched the floor. But I wasn't ready to tell him that yet.

Honest Larry walked out to meet us. We exchanged pleasantries with him, and I glanced around at the cars. The silver Mustang made all the others in the lot look like scrap metal. I'd bought my first car for safety, same reason I'd taken the teaching job. Now I was finally ready to step out on faith a little bit, take a chance. The Mustang was a step.

"Wanna drive her?"

"Hmm?" I looked at Larry. He and Alex were both watching me.

"What? The Mustang?" I smiled, trying hard for nonchalant, but I could tell by Alex's knowing grin I'd missed the mark. "Sure, I'll take her for a spin."

Less than two hours later, I drove away happy in my new-to-me silver Mustang.

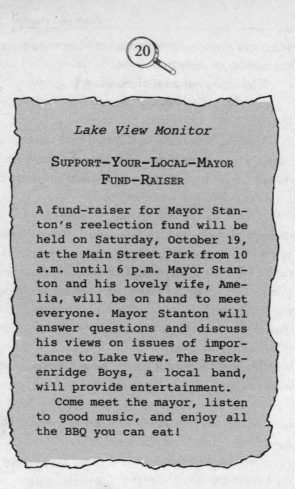

20

Lake View Monitor

Support—Your—Local—Mayor Fund—Raiser

A fund-raiser for Mayor Stanton's reelection fund will be held on Saturday, October 19, at the Main Street Park from 10 a.m. until 6 p.m. Mayor Stanton and his lovely wife, Amelia, will be on hand to meet everyone. Mayor Stanton will answer questions and discuss his views on issues of importance to Lake View. The Breckenridge Boys, a local band, will provide entertainment.

Come meet the mayor, listen to good music, and enjoy all the BBQ you can eat!

I tucked my legs up under me on the couch and looked at the letter again.

Dear Pru,
My house is a mess, my kids are rude,

*and my husband doesn't appreciate me. But
today for a few minutes, we were outside
raking leaves and the love was as tangible
as the cold rake handle. Should I take advantage of those times to talk about how
awful it is the rest of the time? Or just leave
well enough alone?*

Unsure.

After we'd gotten the car, Alex had left his truck at my house and followed me over to Mama and Daddy's in Mama's Buick. Everyone ran out to see my new car, and we'd all teased Zac mercilessly for asking first thing if he could borrow it. When Alex and I were leaving, my parents and Carly and her kids stood on the big front porch for a few minutes, laughing and talking, enjoying one of those simple times that you want to freeze and replay over and over. I'd leaned against the porch rail and silently thanked God for the love He'd given us all.

I thought of that as I penned my reply:

Dear Unsure,
*Sometimes, even in the midst of chaos,
you have to grab little moments of peace
and happiness wherever you can get them.
I'd find a blank-slate time, like first thing
in the morning, to discuss your problems.
Let life's joys be spontaneous and unham-
pered. Peace to you and yours.*

I picked up another letter. I'd started with an easy one, but they seemed a little more difficult to answer this week. Maybe my mind was just too distracted. I reached for the folder of archive letters I'd brought home the first week. A refresher in how the preceding Dear Prus answered might help. I flipped through the questions and snappy answers. Snappy was cute, but sometimes it was too close to snippy. Besides, I wanted to develop my own style.

I started to close the folder when the bright yellow brochure that Carly and I had seen earlier caught my attention. I picked it up.

Makeover for Couples!

Two-for-One Special at the Luxury Spa in Memphis Thursday, September 5 through Sunday, September 8!

Surprise your Special Someone with a spa weekend featuring Botox and collagen injections in the privacy of your Luxury suite with your own personal attendant.

Tanning beds, permanent makeup, and elimination of spider veins and unsightly age spots included.

No need to grow old together gracefully when you can stay young for each other forever.

Something bothered me about that brochure. I just couldn't put my finger on it. The dates were long past.

I glanced at them again. Actually, the dates included the day Hank was murdered. Had Hank considered doing this with Marge and then not gone through with it? If he had, it might have saved his life. Somehow I couldn't imagine him and Marge with tautly stretched skin and full-lipped smiles. That was more up Byron and Amelia's alley.

Of course. Their stiff smiles at the funeral. Amelia's perfect makeup. My thought that they were plastic. They must have been doing little procedures here and there for a long time. Even Hank's upcoming editorial about the mayor being up to his eyebrows in something was a clue. I touched the brochure. Hank must have figured out they were going and intended to rat them out in the paper when they returned.

It wasn't worth killing someone to keep a few beauty secrets, though. Then it hit me. This wasn't the motive. This was their alibi. And I knew John well enough to know he'd checked their story out thoroughly. If I could verify I was right, I could mark them off the suspect list and narrow the field considerably.

I glanced at the clock. Almost nine on a Friday night. John and Denise might have already put the kids to bed, but they'd still be up. I could call. Or I could just drop by and show them my new car. A lame excuse maybe, but at least it was an excuse.

Before I could change my mind, I sped down Liberty Road, past the ruins of Brendan's house, and peered through the darkness at the hulking shell. This case seemed to have more questions than answers.

At John and Denise's, I pulled into the driveway and ran up to the door before I changed my mind.

Denise answered the door. "Jenna, it's good to see you." She hugged me. "Come in."

"I wanted to show y'all my new car."

She clapped her hands together. "Oh, goody! We were finishing up the dishes, but that sounds like loads more fun. John!" she called over her shoulder. "Come see Jenna's new car!"

John actually had a dishcloth in his hand when he came to the kitchen door. Seeing him at home, out of uniform, made me realize how much I'd hated being on the outs with him. "Hey, John, how's it going?"

"Fine. What's this about a new car?"

I shrugged. "Well, it's new to me. Y'all want to come out and see it?"

We walked together out to the car, where I'd conveniently parked under a streetlight. They oohed and aahed over it and patted me on the back. When we got back to the house, Denise turned to me. "Wanna come in for a while?"

"Sure." They were bound to be wondering why I was here. As soon as we got in the foyer, I said, "John, I just wanted to talk to you about Byron and Amelia's alibi."

"Jenna?" John rubbed his hand down his face. "You know I can't answer any questions about that. I've told you a thousand times to butt out. Mind. Your. Own. Business." All of John's words seemed to start with capital letters these days.

"John," Denise gasped. "You can't talk to Jenna that way. You'll hurt her feelings."

"I don't have any questions. I have an answer." I shoved the Luxury Spa brochure into his unwilling hand.

One look at his face was enough to know I'd guessed right. Amelia and Byron had been living in the lap of Luxury the day Hank died.

21

Lake View Monitor

CRIMESTOPPERS NEIGHBORHOOD WATCH

In light of recent happenings, the citizens of Lake View have started a Neighborhood Watch program. For more information or to start a group in your neighborhood, call Debbie at (870) 555-3111.

If Carly had known I'd even considered that Marge might be the murderer, she'd never have agreed to keep Lois occupied while I went to see the widow. But during my sleepless night after I left John and Denise's, my mind had run the gamut of theories. Maybe Hank was killed because of a land deal gone bad or so Marge could collect the insurance. Then I'd thought about Brendan. The only thing I could see that tied the two murder victims together was the pills. It just made sense to see what Marge could tell me about whatever story Hank was doing.

We split up with a plan. Carly would go visit Lois

and keep her from showing up at Marge's. My smart-thinking sister even called ahead to make sure Lois stayed home. I, on the other hand, wanted the element of surprise on my side when I confronted Marge.

So I pulled into Marge's driveway, killed my motor, and slipped quietly up to the door. And rang the doorbell. I wasn't going to break in. But as I stood on the porch, I had that feeling of déjà vu all over again. Hopefully the old saying about the third time being a charm was true.

"Jenna, honey, come in!" She looked genuinely happy to see me. Would she still be glad after she figured out why I was there?

"Hi, Marge. I just wanted to stop by and check on you." *See if maybe you killed your husband.* My throat was so dry I could hardly get my words out.

"I'm glad you did. I'm doing so much better. Come on in and have a seat."

I followed her into the living room and sat down again on the chintz sofa. "You look like you are feeling better."

"I really am."

"I have a question."

"About Dear Pru?"

Her words jarred loose another wild theory I'd had in the night. "Well, I do have a question about Dear Pru, actually. Is it possible that whoever was Dear Pru before me might have been angry enough about getting fired to kill Hank?"

"Oh my, no." Marge shook her head. "Why would you ask?"

"Well, it just seemed odd, him getting killed so soon after the turnover of Dear Pru. The police thought Zac was a suspect because Hank fired him. I just thought maybe this person might be a suspect, too."

"Definitely not."

"In that case, I'll get to the real question I wanted to ask."

"What is it, dear?"

"When I was at the newspaper, I found some pill bottles in a bag. They had women's names on them." She didn't say anything, and I wasn't sure if it was my imagination or if she'd gone a shade whiter. "Those names I asked you and Lois about at church the other day, remember?"

Marge's face crumpled. I'd hoped for some kind of reaction—an eyelid twitch, a facial tic, but I'd never expected this. She looked up at me, tears tracing through the wrinkle track of her face. "You know, don't you?"

"Know? About what?"

"About my problem."

Her problem? Her problem. Of course. I should have seen it earlier. Marge was an addict. "I'm sorry." I patted her on the back.

She shook her head and snatched a Kleenex from the box next to her. "I don't care, I don't care. I was terrified Hank would find out. But he did anyway right before he died." She blew her nose loudly. "I'd have checked into rehab after that, but Lois said it would look suspicious. She was worried that the police would arrest me because I didn't have an alibi."

"What about Lois's stomach bug?"

"Truth is—I was passed out from the drugs. That's why I didn't know Hank wasn't home. Lois made the other up to protect me."

"She's a good friend."

"Yes, she is. She cared for me after my back surgery, and when the pain was so bad, she understood that I had to have my pills. Since then, she's tried everything to help me quit the drugs, but I couldn't."

"Are you still using?" I asked quietly.

She shook her head. "I took myself off cold turkey after the funeral. It almost killed me."

I remembered the haunted look in her eyes on my second visit when she'd said she'd rather live with the pain than lose herself. She'd been speaking from hard experience. "I'm sorry," I told her. I paused for a few seconds. "So who were the women whose names were on the bottles?"

"Oh, they weren't real people. After my prescription ran out, Lois talked Brendan into selling me pills under fake names. Just until I could quit."

"I guess Hank was pretty mad at Brendan when he found out."

Marge nodded. "Listen, if Hank hadn't been dead when Brendan died, I'd have thought Hank killed him. That's how mad he was."

I stood and hugged her. "I'm glad you got it under control, Marge. I'll be praying you keep getting better."

"Thank you, Jenna. I'll be praying you get the answers you're looking for, too."

"Thanks."

As soon as I was in the car, I called Carly's cell phone. No answer. I wanted to ask Lois some questions anyway, so I headed in that direction. As I drove along the river road, I glanced out at the sparkling water down below. Saturdays should be spent kayaking or fishing, not interrogating sweet elderly women so I could find a murderer.

I breathed a prayer of thanks that Marge had broken free from the drug habit. It would have been so much easier on her if she'd only gotten help. I could understand her not wanting to while Hank was alive in case he found out, but it looked like Lois would have insisted after his death. If Marge had been honest with John about her alibi, he'd have understood.

I turned down the little lane that led to Lois's riverfront house. The alibi. It hadn't only been Marge's alibi; it had been Lois's, as well. Unless I missed my guess, Lois had hated Hank. He'd been talking to Brendan about the drugs. No doubt he'd discovered that Lois had gotten Marge the pills from Brendan. My mind whirled like the river currents below. According to Marge, Lois was the main one who dealt with Brendan. Had she dealt with him permanently?

This was my most unbelievable scenario yet, but what if I was right and Carly was entertaining a murderer? Carly's van loomed ahead in Lois's driveway. I picked up my phone and punched in Carly's number again. No answer. I hesitated, then dialed John.

"John? It's Jenna." I started telling him about

Marge and Lois, but he interrupted me.

"Jenna, I'm worried about you. I think maybe you should get some counseling."

"I—" The line was dead. I punched in 9-1. Then stopped. Was I prepared to go into an innocent woman's house and have it surrounded by police within minutes? Did I really want to face that kind of humiliation?

I hit the END button on my phone and climbed out of the car, praying as I walked up to the house. Carly's old van was parked in the driveway. And the front door was open. I could hear voices through the screen door. Suddenly Lois stepped onto the porch. "Jenna, come in, come in. I'm so glad to see you." She looked so innocent in her polyester slacks and oversized cardigan. Like everybody's grandma. But something in her eyes wasn't right.

I froze and weighed my choices. Run as fast as I could in the opposite direction or go in and join Carly in the black widow's web. Not very good options. But I wasn't about to desert my sister. "Hi, I just thought I'd drop by." I forced a smile that must have looked more like a grimace.

"Actually, I was about to call you. Carly's bored with me, I'm afraid."

When I entered the house, it took a few seconds for my eyes to adjust from the bright sunlight to the dim interior. But there was Carly at the kitchen table, a cup of coffee in front of her. She had her elbow on the tiled surface and her hand under her chin. "Hi, Shenna. Jenna," she mumbled. "Good to shee you." Her eyelids drooped.

I glanced at Lois, who was smiling. "Let me pour you a cup of coffee, dear."

"No, thanks. I just came to get Carly. Emergency at home." I walked over to my sister and nudged her. Her elbow fell out from under her chin, and she barely got it back under her before her face splatted against the table. I wanted to scream.

"I'm sorry to hear there's an emergency." Lois didn't move to stop me, just stood there smiling with her hands in her cardigan pockets.

"Emerg—emergensheee?" Carly slurred the word and shook her head.

"Yeah, Car, we have to get home." I grabbed her arm and tried to pull her up. "Now."

"You have to drink some coffee with me before you go, Jenna," Lois said.

"No, thank you," I said firmly.

Then she raised her hand from her pocket, and I found myself staring down the barrel of a lethal-looking pistol. "I insist." She motioned to the chair next to Carly. "Have a seat."

I sat down at the table. "Is this what you did to Hank? Held a gun on him and made him drink coffee?"

She laughed. "You've been reading too many mysteries if you think you can keep me talking long enough to escape. I'm a librarian, remember?" She plunked a dainty white and blue coffee cup in front of me then leaned in close to me. "I've read them all. There's no way out for you, Jenna. You've asked one too many questions. Even the chief of police thinks you're crazy."

She picked up the pot from the counter and poured my coffee, then kept her eye on me as she brazenly poured some white powder into it. "Drink."

"What's in it?"

"What difference does it make?"

"I'd rather know what kind of death I'm facing."

"I'm not into rat poison. Just something to make you relax."

Carly's arm gave way, and the weight of her head plopped onto the tabletop. I reached for her, but Lois motioned toward the coffee with the gun. "Drink or die now."

I leaned toward Carly anyway and was quiet until I could hear her light snoring. Sitting up straight, I looked at Lois. "I'll drink if you'll tell me why you did it. Surely I deserve to know that much."

She narrowed her eyes as if to gauge my sincerity, then nodded. "Take a drink."

I took a swig from the coffee cup and watched with a little satisfaction as her eyes widened. She'd been expecting ladylike sips, no doubt. "So talk."

She sat down across from me, gun above the table, trained on me. "Men are a problem, dear. In a way, I'm doing you a favor by keeping you from having to deal with them anymore."

"You'll forgive me if I don't thank you," I murmured, fury warring with pure fear inside my chest.

She laughed. "I learned early enough that when you have a problem with men, you have to get rid of them. It worked with my dad and then with my husband.

Marge is the only one who ever understood me."

The woman was stark-raving mad. And the fact that John would feel terribly guilty at my and Carly's double funeral gave me no comfort at all. I looked around the room for a sharp object, even a blunt object. If I could distract her for a second. . .

"Take another drink." She was staring at me intently. No doubt she knew exactly what I was thinking. I picked up the cup and drank. Black coffee. Yuck. But whatever she'd put in it was tasteless.

"Did Hank know the coffee was drugged?"

She shook her head. "He had no idea. A nice cup of fresh-brewed coffee—my little way of making it up to him for threatening to keep Marge away from me. The golf club wasn't necessary, but it helped me feel better about his firing me from Dear Pru."

I gasped.

She laughed. "You didn't guess? See? I was good at it. If the golf pro hadn't been such a big baby. . ." She shook her head and clucked her tongue. "Hank had to die."

"What about Brendan?"

She looked at me and tilted her head.

I faked a yawn and was rewarded with a big smile from her. "How'd you get him to drink coffee with you?" My words were slurred. Not too much, but enough to buy me some time.

"I thought Brendan was different at first. One of those rare good men. He didn't seem to have a problem helping Marge with her pain medicine as long as the payments kept coming. But then he started figuring things out after Hank's death. And you kept asking questions. So I held a gun on him and he wrote the note, then drank his coffee just like you are." Her smile was gone. "Only he went out fast like your sister."

I shuddered and looked at Carly's cup. Hers was barely touched. Mine was half gone. How much more could I take?

"It was painless. He was unconscious when the fire started. Take another drink." Her voice had changed and the smile was gone. Should I pretend to pass out on the table? Or was her idea of painless death to knock us out with drugs then put a bullet through our skulls? I couldn't chance it.

I reached for my cup but missed on purpose and yawned again.

She pushed to her feet. "Good. It's finally kicking in." She waved the gun at me, and I braced myself for the shot. "Come on and help me with your sister while you can still stand."

She put one arm under Carly's, but I remained seated. No need to make it easy for her.

The gun barrel shifted to Carly. "She's deadweight anyway. Doesn't matter to me if she's just plain dead. Nobody will notice the gunshot by the time her body washes to shore."

I stood quickly but then remembered the drugs should be affecting me. I moved to Carly's other side, stumbling as I went. "To shore?" I asked, slurring the words.

"Yeah, you're going to have another little car accident. Only this time your dear sister is going to drive you into the river." She heaved Carly up, and I helped. Our chances of getting away would surely be better outside. And had she forgotten I was a swimmer? It would be tough, but I had a better-than-average chance of rescuing us. *If* the pills didn't kick in.

I knew from past experience that when the pills took effect, it would happen all at once. In my mind, I kept a stream of prayers going up, asking for that moment not to be too soon. Carly had conveniently parked the van facing straight toward the river bluff. Nothing would stop two sleepy sisters from plunging to their death. And how long would it be before anyone even knew we were missing?

Too soon we were at the van, and Lois leaned Carly against the side and opened the driver's door.

"Lois!"

Startled, Lois turned. Marge stood there in the driveway. I threw myself against Lois. Her gun went flying, and she tumbled to the ground with Carly and me in her wake. Thankfully, Lois landed on bottom. I looked up to see Marge holding the gun.

Lois scrambled to her feet, knocking Carly and me into the grass. "What are you going to do? Shoot me?" she taunted Marge.

"Try me," Marge said grimly. "Just try me."

Lois's eyes widened. "Hank was going to keep us apart. He was so mad at me for helping you get pills. He said I'd never see you again."

"I wouldn't have let that happen." Tears trickled down Marge's face, but the gun in her hand never wavered.

"I did it for you, Marge. I did it all for you."

Sirens sounded in the distance.

"Save it for the judge," Marge said then looked down at me. "You all right, honey?"

"I'm sheep—sleepy." I fought to get up but couldn't lift my head.

"It's too late for her. She's had enough roofies to kill a horse." Lois laughed. "At least I'll have the satisfaction of knowing I took care of Miss Nosy before they got me."

The world was fading to black, but I had time to breathe one more prayer. *Dear God, please let her be wrong.*

22

> *Lake View Monitor*
>
> ### HELP WANTED
>
> Lake View Library seeks
> stable, easygoing librar-
> ian to fill immediate open-
> ing. Send your résumé ASAP
> to P.O. Box 183338, Lake
> View, AR 72001.

Beyond the intense beam of light, everything was white. I could hear. . .singing? No. More monotonous. *Beep. Beep.*

A cool hand touched my forehead. If I could just keep my eyes open long enough to focus.

"She's waking up." Mama sounded happy.

My dad's face floated in front of me. "Jenna, Jenna, honey, how do you feel?"

"Are you in heaven with me?" Even to me, my voice sounded strange.

"Honey, you're in the hospital, not in heaven." Mama's laugh sounded like a sob.

"Hospital?" That explained the tiredness.

She looked at Daddy. "Do you want to go out and tell the others she's awake?"

He nodded then gave me a big hug. Then right there at my bedside, my quiet dad took my hand and closed his eyes. "Dear Lord, thank You so much for giving us our baby back." When he opened his eyes, tears were glistening there.

Whatever happened to me, I must have been at death's door. After he went out, I said as much to Mama, who was bustling around, getting me some clothes to put on and laying out my toothbrush and toothpaste.

"We had some scary times, sweetie. The whole church family has been praying for you around the clock, though."

"What happened to me?"

She walked over to my bedside and used the arrows to raise me to a sitting position. "How much do you remember?"

Remembering was a strain, but the events of that Saturday came back to me slowly. "Lois drugged me."

Mama nodded.

"And Carly!" I looked around the room. "Where's Carly? Is she okay?" I threw the covers back and started to swing my legs down.

"Wait, wait!" Mama put her hand on my legs. "Carly's fine. She slept for about twelve hours and woke up. You've been out of it for three days. But Carly has no memory of anything once she got to Lois's."

Relief sapped me of any desire to get up. I sank back against the mattress. "Why do I remember?"

"We didn't know if you would or not. Your reaction

to this drug isn't typical." Her smile was watery. "But then, you've never been typical." She nodded toward the hairbrush on the bedside table. "A lot of people want to see you. Why don't we get you freshened up a little?"

Why don't we not and say we did? All I really wanted to do was just go back to sleep.

"Alex is in the hall, waiting his turn to come in."

In that case. . . I slid my legs around again, and this time she let me.

A few minutes later, my breath minty fresh, I sat in the blue vinyl chair next to the bed while Mama brushed my hair. "Your daddy and I have been so worried. Jenna Marie, promise me you won't ever pull a stunt like this again. Confronting that crazy woman. And it's not enough that you go, but to get Carly to go, too! You girls could've been killed!" When she noticed the tears streaming down my cheeks, she stopped. She buried her face in my hair and wrapped her arms around me. "Jenna, honey, you girls are our lives. If we lost you. . .well, it's just unthinkable. I didn't mean to upset you; I'm just so thankful you're okay."

I twisted around to meet her hug. I felt so safe in Mama's arms. But, I guess partly because of the lingering effects of the drug, I couldn't stop crying. Face buried in Mama's shoulder, I mourned everything, from losing the Olympics to losing Colton. And for misplacing Alex. I cried for my inadequacies. I had messed up enough for someone twice my age. When I thought of what a blessing it was to have a Father in heaven who forgave my inadequacies, in addition to earthly parents who loved me for who I was, I cried some more. After the tears were gone, I pushed back and patted Mama's soggy shoulder. "Sorry."

"This old thing?" She motioned toward her turquoise blouse. "Don't give it another thought. Do you feel better?"

I nodded. I really did. "Think I've got time for a shower?"

"You've got all the time in the world, honey." That was good to know. I looked forward to heaven. But I was happy living the life on earth God had planned for me. Including the twists and turns.

After my shower, Mama settled me back into the blue chair.

"Knock, knock." I looked up to see Alex standing in the door, unshaven and wrinkled but, I had no doubt, still the best-looking man in the hospital.

"Hey."

"Hey, water girl." He dropped a light kiss on my brow. I hurried to unpucker my lips before he saw me. *Somebody let me out of the hospital!* We were regressing. "How you doing?"

"I'm doing okay. Slowly putting the pieces together."

He took my hand. "We thought we were going to lose you for a while there."

I reached up with my other hand and rubbed the stubble on his cheek. "Have you been staying here?"

"Yes." He shrugged. "They had to sneak me into ICU." He shot me a wry grin. "Since we don't have an official relationship."

"Leave it to a lawyer to worry about legalities. Official or not, I missed you."

In my mind, I interrogated him. *Counselor Campbell, did you mean you want an official relationship with the patient? Or not? If so, what constitutes an official relationship in your mind?*

"Jenna? Did you hear me?"

I looked up to see a worried look in Alex's eyes.

"Sorry. I was just thinking. What did you say?"

"I said I missed you, too." He bent down and hugged me as if I were made of spun glass. Yes, it was definitely time to check out of the hospital. "I'd better go and let the others come in."

I reluctantly let go of his hand.

Carly was my next visitor. When I told her all the things Lois had said, she was disappointed that she'd slept through it. "I barely remember that Saturday at all," she said, shaking her head.

"Car?" I threaded my fingers through hers.

"Yeah?"

"I'm sorry for getting you into this mess."

She laughed. "Are you kidding me? I wouldn't have missed it for anything." She squeezed my hand. "You bring out the best in me, kiddo. I can't believe I was brave enough to help solve a murder."

"I couldn't have done it without you." I looked over her shoulder. "Who's got the twins?"

"Zac's watching them." She smiled. "Here's a news flash. Hayley and Rachel have hardly been fighting at all since Saturday. Something about almost losing us must have made them appreciate a little more what they have."

"I'm so glad, Carly."

"Me, too. Not that I necessarily expect it to last." She hugged me. "I've got to go. Marge has been sitting out there waiting to talk to you ever since Daddy called and told her you woke up."

"Oh, okay." I clutched Carly's arm. "Is she mad at me for ruining her life?"

Carly gave me a you-must-be-crazy look. "Honey, don't develop a phobia about sweet little ladies, okay?" She smiled. "She's not mad at you." She kissed me on the cheek and left me to face Marge alone.

"Jenna, honey. I'm so sorry." Marge hugged me, tears streaming. "Are you sure you're okay?"

"I'm okay. And I'm sorry, too." I patted her back. How could she be thinking of me when she'd gone through so much? "I'm so thankful you showed up at Lois's."

"I couldn't really believe it was true. But I had to find out for myself."

"Marge, this must be awful for you."

"It's been tough. But Amelia and Byron are staying with me a few days."

I must have looked as stunned as I felt, because she actually laughed through the tears.

"She and I are working things out, believe it or not. Come by and see me, and I'll tell you all about it."

"I'll do that." If I hadn't been so tired, I'd have made her tell me right then.

"Thanks, Jenna. I appreciate your getting to the bottom of all this." She hugged me again, in a cloud of spearmint.

I relaxed my head against the chair back and closed my eyes.

"How about a nap?" Mama said from the doorway.

"Sounds good."

She tucked me in and sat down beside me. I drifted off to sleep, safe in the knowledge that, as crazy as this world gets, I have a place in it.

Over the next twenty-four hours, visitors poured in the door, some out of concern, some out of just plain curiosity. Between Mama, Daddy, Alex, and Carly, I hardly had to talk to anyone. They just said, "The police have asked us not to share any details." Bob brought me a box of chocolates, but it didn't take him but a minute to ask me when I could come back to work. To hear him tell it, the place was falling apart without me there.

The king and queen of Lake View stopped by for a short visit. While Byron was talking to Daddy, I asked Amelia about Marge. "Byron and I have been staying with her ever since Lois was arrested. Come by and visit her when you get out." I was dying of curiosity to get to the bottom of that. Guess I hadn't learned my lesson. Let's hope this cat has nine lives.

John and Denise came, with flowers, and I half expected an apology. Instead, I got the usual speech about minding my own business and staying out of police investigations. But when, at the end of the speech, they both hugged me and John said, "I'm so glad you're okay, Jenna," I could tell he really meant it.

He even grudgingly shared some information with me. Lois was spilling her guts to anyone who would listen. Evaluations were under way, but it looked like she might not be mentally competent enough to stand trial. She did say she felt bad about trying to kill Carly, but she apparently had few regrets about "Miss Nosy." If I hadn't had such a close brush with death, I'm pretty sure John would have smiled when he told me that. Before I could remind him that if not for me, a murderer would be walking free, Doc Brown stuck his head in the door, and John and Denise left.

"Young lady, you need to try and stay out of trouble. I don't want to see you back here again for a long time." Doc Brown had been my doctor for as long as I could remember and still talked to me as if I were a child. "It doesn't look like you're going to have any long-lasting effects from those drugs." After shining that bright light in my eyes one more time, he sent me home. "I think you're clear to resume your normal activities." He winked at me. "As long as that doesn't include trying to catch a murderer."

The day after I got home from the hospital, I was on Marge's front porch—again. Grief covered her like a mantle, but along with it was a quiet strength I'd never seen in her. "Oh, Jenna, honey, come in. I'm so glad you came over." I gave her a hug and was relieved to feel her ribs weren't as prominent. Maybe she was slowly getting her life back together, too. "Is Amelia still staying with you?"

"No, she and Byron went back home. They wanted me to move in with them, but I'm not ready to leave my house yet. So many good memories here." She glanced around the living room.

"I'm sure there are." I hoped I sounded comforting, like Mama.

She gestured toward the sofa, and we both sat down. "I blame myself for all of this. If I had only known about Lois's feelings, maybe I could have helped her." Marge's eyes were full of gut-wrenching sadness. "But after my back surgery, I was in such pain. She moved in for a while to help me. Then I got hooked on pain medicine. . . ." She gave me a wry smile.

I could easily imagine Lois subtly encouraging Marge to become dependent on the pain meds, but I saw no purpose in sharing that suspicion with Marge.

"And after that, things were pretty much a blur. I relied on her for everything." She shook her head. "I had no idea her mind was so. . .twisted."

I patted her on the shoulder. "No one could tell anything was wrong. She seemed normal."

"So you and Amelia have worked out your differences?" I didn't want to sound like a gossip buzzard waiting to swoop down, but I just had to know.

She nodded. "After Lois was arrested and I began to realize the depths of her deception, I called Amelia.

We had our first heart-to-heart in decades." She patted my hand. "When I tell you this, you'll just have to forgive me for being so gullible. I'd been friends with Lois since childhood. That's my only excuse."

"You trusted her. That's to be expected." I hated to see her feel guilt on top of everything else. She hadn't been to blame.

"When Byron and Amelia were newly married, Lois told Hank and me that Byron had made a pass at her. I know you young people may find it hard to believe, but Lois was a beauty in her day." Marge's voice grew distant, as if she were looking way back into the past. "We were both furious and wanted to tell Amelia, but Lois didn't want to cause trouble in Amelia's marriage. Hank never liked Byron after that, and he didn't want me around him, either."

"I can understand that." Hank may have been cranky, but he had morals.

"Over the next few years, Lois would mention that Byron tried to get her to go away with him for a weekend when he went out of town on business. Or that he tried to get her into a secluded area at a public get-together." Marge shook her head. "Of course I told Hank every time. Eventually Hank would use his power in town to fight Byron on every corner. After that, Hank and Byron were sworn enemies. I wanted to tell Amelia, but she was obviously so much in love with Byron that I was afraid it would destroy her. I kept waiting to hear rumors about him being unfaithful to her, but in all these years I haven't heard a thing." She closed her eyes. "That should have told me something."

"You couldn't have known."

She opened her eyes and looked at me as if she'd forgotten I was there. "It was all lies. Did you know that? Every bit of it. They let me go see Lois the other day, and she couldn't wait to confirm that she'd made the whole thing up. She also bragged that every time it looked like Amelia and I might make up, she'd invent something that she'd heard Amelia said about me."

"Oh, Marge, I'm so sorry." I couldn't imagine losing all those years with Carly. "But you've got each other now."

Marge smiled, a little of the haunted look gone from her eyes. "Yes, we do. And we intend to make the most of that." Amelia was picking her up for lunch in a few minutes, so I hugged her and left, with a promise to visit often.

Marge and Amelia weren't the only ones who were making up for lost time. I had to get ready for a date of my own.

When sisters **Christine Pearle Lynxwiler**, **Jan Pearle Reynolds**, and **Sandy Pearle Gaskin** came up with the idea for a Chrisitan cozy mystery series during Sunday dinner at Mama's, they determined to take their dream further than just table talk. Thus the Sleuthing Sisters mystery series was born.

Christine writes full-time. She and her husband, Kevin, live with their two children in the beautiful Ozark Mountains and enjoy kayaking on the nearby Spring River. Jan, part-time writer and full-time office manager, and her husband, Steve, love to spend time with their two adult children and their granddogs on the lake or just relaxing at home. Sandy, part-time writer and retired teacher, works with her husband, Bart, managing their manufacturing business. She spends her spare time shuttling their teenager back and forth to school activities. But knowing how quickly these days will be gone, she wouldn't have it any other way.

You may correspond with these authors by writing:
Author Relations
PO Box 721
Uhrichsville, Oh 44683

A Letter to Our Readers

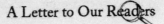

Dear Reader:
In order to help us satisfy your quest for more great mystery stories, we would appreciate it if you would take a few minutes to respond to the following questions. We welcome your comments and read each form and letter we receive. When completed, please return to:

Fiction Editor
Heartsong Presents—MYSTERIES!
PO Box 721
Uhrichsville, Ohio 44683

Did you enjoy reading *Death on a Deadline* by Sandy Gaskin, Christine Lynxwiler, and Jan Reynolds?

Very much! I would like to see more books like this!
The one thing I particularly enjoyed about this story was:

_____

_____

_____

Moderately. I would have enjoyed it more if:

_____

_____

_____

Are you a member of the HP—MYSTERIES! Book Club?
Yes   No

If no, where did you purchase this book?

_____

Please rate the following elements using a scale of 1 (poor) to 10 (superior):

___ Main character/sleuth   ___ Romance elements

___ Inspirational theme   ___ Secondary characters

___ Setting   ___ Mystery plot

How would you rate the cover design on a scale of 1 (poor) to 5 (superior)? _____

What themes/settings would you like to see in future **Heartsong Presents—MYSTERIES!** selections? _____
_____
_____
_____

Please check your age range:
- ◯ Under 18   ◯ 18–24
- ◯ 25–34   ◯ 35–45
- ◯ 46–55   ◯ Over 55

Name: _____

Occupation: _____

Address: _____

E-mail address: _____